"Tell me the truth, Jessie,"

Ben asked. He dragged a hand over his face, then stifled a groan. He'd forgotten his skin was still sensitive where he'd scraped it. "Jessie . . . do I look half as frightening as I feel?"

"Now who's fishing for compliments?"

He followed her low, melodious voice. "Everyone keeps saying I shouldn't worry but . . . my nose is broken and I seem to have stitches everywhere."

"Stop exaggerating," Jessie scoffed lightly. "Look at it this way, you were too darned handsome for your own good anyway."

Ben had to remind himself that grown men didn't pout. "You used to say I looked noble."

"What did you expect? When you were my doctor, I thought you were a white knight. Anyway, the worst injury is the blow to the back of your head."

"Wrong," Ben snapped at Jessie. "The worst injury is that I can't *see*. . . ."

Dear Reader,

The summer is over, it's back to school and time to look forward to the delights of autumn—the changing leaves, the harvest, the special holidays... and those frosty nights curled up by the fire with a Silhouette Romance novel.

Silhouette Romance books always reflect the laughter, the tears, the sheer joy of falling in love. And this month is no exception as our heroines find the heroes of their dreams—from the boy next door to the handsome, mysterious stranger.

September continues our WRITTEN IN THE STARS series. Each month in 1991, we're proud to present a book that focuses on the hero—and his astrological sign. September features the strong, enticingly reserved Virgo man in Helen R. Myers's *Through My Eyes*.

I hope you enjoy this month's selection of stories, and in the months to come, watch for Silhouette Romance novels by your all-time favorites including Diana Palmer, Brittany Young, Annette Broadrick and many others.

We love to hear from our readers, and we'd love to hear from *you!*

Happy Reading,

Valerie Susan Hayward
Senior Editor

HELEN R. MYERS

Through My Eyes

Silhouette Romance

Published by Silhouette Books New York

America's Publisher of Contemporary Romance

Author's Note

To my Readers:
Research indicates that two-person paddle boats are no longer in use down on the River Walk; however, for purposes of nostalgia, I brought them back for this story.

SILHOUETTE BOOKS
300 E. 42nd St., New York, N.Y. 10017

THROUGH MY EYES

ISBN: 0-373-08814-0

First Silhouette Books printing September 1991

Books by Helen R. Myers

Silhouette Romance

Donovan's Mermaid #557
Someone to Watch Over Me #643
Confidentially Yours #677
Invitation to a Wedding #737
A Fine Arrangement #776
Through My Eyes #814

Silhouette Desire

Partners for Life #370
Smooth Operator #454
That Fontaine Woman! #471
The Pirate O'Keefe #506
Kiss Me Kate #570
After You #599
When Gabriel Called #650

HELEN R. MYERS

lives on a sixty-five-acre ranch deep in the piney woods of East Texas with her husband, Robert, and a constantly expanding menagerie. She lists her interests as everything that doesn't have to do with a needle and thread. When she and Robert aren't working on the house they've built together, she likes to read, garden and, of course, outfish her husband.

A NOTE FROM THE AUTHOR
Dear Reader,

As a Scorpio, I've long accepted my fascination
about every mystery regarding life and death, and
that includes my curiosity about astrology.
Therefore, I was thrilled with the invitation to
participate in the WRITTEN IN THE STARS series.

Creating Dr. Benedict Collier was my first
opportunity to take a closer look at the sign of Virgo.
I saw Ben as an all-around "nice guy," but totally
dedicated to his profession—the type who's often
overshadowed by more charismatic or macho men.
The life partner I wanted for him was someone who
knew her own mind (and his) well enough to show
him that all work and no play made Ben a lonely
guy. And so Taurean Jessica Holland came along to
serve above and beyond the call of duty.

Ben and Jessie charmed me. I hope you enjoy their
story, too.

Helen R. Myers

Chapter One

On his seventh day in the hospital, Benedict Collier discovered that oatmeal, when allowed to cool and then flung across the room, was inclined to cling to a wall for a considerable length of time before dropping to the tile floor in a series of muffled thumps. Compared to the information days one through six had provided him, it was enlightenment of unparalleled proportions.

Naturally, the mess was going to put someone in a foul mood, but that didn't make Ben feel overly repentant. After all, things might have been worse, since technically he'd been hoping to connect with a window. The problem was he didn't even know if he was in a room that had a window.

As if on cue, terror rose out of nowhere and raced through him like a runaway freight train, crushing his anger and leaving him shaking. Once again he could do little more than grip his bed sheet and silently repeat the litany he'd been soothing himself with ever since he'd regained consciousness and realized he was imprisoned in a world of darkness that wasn't artificial; that the bandages swathed around his head came nowhere close to covering his eyes. He would not lose control, he told himself, he would not break down. But, oh God, it was worse than he'd imagined blindness to be. He was scared, and he didn't know how much longer he could keep his fear under control.

Blind. The mere thought of the word made his blood run cold. It sounded so permanent. He, one of San Antonio's leading ophthalmologists, who'd told dozens and dozens of his patients that their conditions weren't necessarily permanent, was now being fed the same line by doctors, his *colleagues*. How empty the token reassurance felt now that it was directed at him. If only Dr. Wescott had come out of surgery sooner last Friday and they'd had their consultation on the Thomas case when they'd originally scheduled it. If only he hadn't stopped in Mr. Grigg's room to listen to a tale about the wiry cowboy's days on the rodeo circuit. So many excuses. He'd never cared for them or the people who used them. Life was full of "if onlys," yet here he was playing the hindsight game like every other poor fool who wouldn't admit he'd helped set himself up for a catastrophe.

The fact remained that last Friday night, at minutes before eleven, *he* had been the one to walk out into the hospital's poorly lit parking lot, and *he* had been the one who'd been beaten and mugged. His assailant hadn't cared that he was making a terrible mistake, that his actions would end the career of one of the city's leading eye specialists. The man had wanted his wallet and instead of allowing Ben to hand it over he'd attacked him, beating him unconscious with some sort of metal object.

It was the story one read about in the papers and heard on the evening news, the kind of tragedy that happened to someone else. And from Ben's perspective, it was also other people who recovered and went back to living normal, productive lives. Deep inside, he had already decided his colleagues—soon to be his former colleagues—could continue reassuring him until they were hoarse, but he knew he wasn't going to be one of the happily ever after cases. He wasn't going to regain his vision.

Under the circumstances, he might as well be dead. The thought was based more on common sense than self-pity...all right, maybe he felt some bitterness, too, but it wasn't without justification. After all, he was thirty-eight, and up until last week, his entire existence had been centered around his work. There weren't enough hours in the day to fit in all the patients there were to see, operations to perform, symposiums to conduct. It never occurred to him that he was missing out on a personal life because there simply had never been time to dwell on it. Now that time was all he had, he could do nothing *but* focus on it, and the prospects he saw for his future in that area weren't pretty either.

Most of all he wondered why—why had his ability to do what he was best at been taken away from him?

What good was he to anyone if he couldn't do what he'd been trained for?

As he asked himself that question for the umpteenth time, a faint sound caught his attention and he stiffened, listened. The door—someone had opened the door slightly. Automatically turning to see who was intruding, he sucked in a sharp breath, momentarily forgetting his blindness and the shooting pain that still followed any abrupt movements. "Go away," he said shakily, as the needlelike sensations receded to a more bearable throb.

There was no answer. He sensed that the intruder was hesitating and that had him tensing again. Who was it this time? He'd been examined, prodded and probed by practically everyone but the resident nutritionist. He thought he'd also convinced people that he'd suffered through more than enough reunions. After he'd been found, someone contacted his parents, who flew in from Phoenix. His younger sister, six months pregnant with her first child, drove down from Dallas with her husband. Though ordinarily Ben felt he had a good relationship with his family, it hadn't been long before he began to feel suffocated by all the attention and forced cheerfulness. Finally he'd been compelled to ask, then demand they go home. When that didn't work, he'd resorted to ignoring them until yesterday when reluctantly they'd relented and left. Apparently the rest of the hospital staff weren't going to be as obliging.

"Whoever you are, I don't intend to talk to you, so you might as well go away."

As if that made up his visitor's mind, Ben heard the door open further. Someone stepped inside, then carefully let the door close behind him. Him? No, the step was too light for a man; Ben was already becoming adept at identifying sounds. When he noticed the floral scent that faintly permeated the hospital's permanent antiseptic smell, he further amended his guess by deciding his visitor was a woman.

No doubt another nurse. She'd probably spotted the oatmeal on the wall and was having second thoughts about whether it was wise to get within firing range. "Don't worry," he muttered, not quite able to repress all his sarcasm, "I'm over my temper tantrum."

He felt more than heard her step closer. That cancelled out his guess that it was Nurse Hodges, who normally shuffled around like a street sweeper and looked as if she could bench press a school bus without breaking into a sweat. However, Hodges was known to make good use of the nurse's aides, and from the springlike scent his visitor was wearing, Ben decided that's who this must be.

"Look, I'm sorry about the mess," he added, trying to put aside his own misery for a moment and be civil. For all he knew she could be one of the candy stripers, and the last thing he needed on his conscience was knowing he'd made a young girl cry. "Just take my tray and—"

Her fragrance...something about it triggered a memory. He knew it, not because he was an expert on perfumes, but because he knew someone who wore it exclusively. Yes...now he remembered. She'd been a patient. Fountain of whimsical information that she

was, she'd informed him that the scent's base was
representative of Taurus and the hyacinth, her astrological sign and flower.

Growing ever more suspicious, Ben thrust out his
hand. "Come here."

He could sense her hesitating again, but after a
moment she came to the side of his bed and placed her
hand in his. Forcing himself to ignore the seemingly
fragile bones beneath smooth, resilient flesh, Ben
gripped it, half expecting her to try to escape once she
discovered what he intended to do.

Yet as he ran his free hand up her bare arm, he
couldn't help note the warmth, the softness of youth-
ful skin...the cuff of a short sleeve he would bet
anything was white. He skimmed his hand over a de-
ceptively slender shoulder and stretched his fingers
toward her nape. There he found a barrette and, at
last, the wild tumble of curls he'd been expecting.
Even so, he abruptly released her as if stung by something trespassing through his darkness, as indeed it
had been.

"So," he murmured tightly, settling back against his
pillows, "they've decided to bring in the big guns."

"No need to get insulting, Doc. You know I'd only
qualify as bantamweight."

For an instant Ben visualized the lithe young woman
who'd walked into his office several years ago looking as if she'd stepped out of a Gothic novel with her
blue-black curls framing a pale, elfin face. Though he
knew she was almost average height, she was right; she
would have to stuff her cheeks like a chipmunk to tip

the scales anywhere close to a hundred and ten pounds. But he didn't want to think about that now.

"What are you doing here, Jessie? Normally you treat me as if I had the bubonic plague."

"Only typhoid, but you can relax. This doesn't have anything to do with that. I just happened to be down the hall talking to Nurse Hodges when we heard the crash in here. She's wearing a new uniform and already had one close call this morning, so I told her I'd take the risk and come see how bad the damage was."

Though her tone was conversational, Ben knew there was probably nothing casual in Jessica Holland's expression as he felt her study his bruised face. There wasn't much he could do about that; but when she gently touched his cheek, he turned his head away.

"I'm glad I could help her out," she continued as if nothing had happened. "She wouldn't have been thrilled with that wall."

Ben didn't bother pretending to be fooled. She wasn't here as a favor to Nurse Hodges any more than she was interested in how much trouble he could get into with the old dragon. "Who talked you into coming to see me, Jessie?"

He wasn't angry, he simply wanted her to know he wasn't about to tolerate any more evasions or fabricated stories. Maybe he couldn't look for the truth in her heavily lashed moss-green eyes, but he would be able to tell by her voice. If he'd learned anything since the time she'd been his patient, it was that she'd never been any good at deception, particularly when it came to hiding her feelings for him. He'd hoped the three years that had passed since she'd regained her own

eyesight, graduated from nursing school and started
a new career, had helped heal the wounds he'd felt it
necessary to inflict as a result of those misplaced feelings. If he was wrong...no, he couldn't face the
prospect that he could be.

"Who?" he demanded, though not unkindly.

She hesitated only a few seconds. "Mar— Dr. Tremaine."

"Tremaine." Ben sucked in a deep, though careful
breath and exhaled wearily. "Count on that lawless
wretch to stick his nose where it's not wanted and turn
loose my favorite ex-patient on me. Well, tell him you
did your best, but that I'm a lost cause, all right?"

"Was I your favorite patient, Doc?"

"Jessie—"

"Oh, all right. But you can't throw me out yet. You
know full well he'd never believe I'd give up this easily."

"Convince him. It's what you're particularly good
at, isn't it?"

As soon as the words were out, Ben regretted them.
One of the reasons Jessie had been his favorite patient was because she possessed an incomparable determination to make things work out for the best. She
was a survivor, someone who would make the most of
her life regardless of whether he'd succeeded with his
operation on her or not. It was just that sometimes,
like now, all that willpower could be damned frus-
trating.

Ben dragged a hand over his face. An instant later
he was stifling a groan, having forgotten that his skin
was still sensitive where he'd bruised and scraped it on

the pavement. "Jessie . . . do I look half as frightening as I feel I do?"

"Now who's fishing for compliments?"

He followed her low, melodious voice with blind eyes. "Tell me the truth. Everyone keeps saying I shouldn't worry about a few bumps and bruises, but my fingers tell me differently. My nose is broken and . . . and I seem to have stitches everywhere."

"Stop exaggerating," she scoffed lightly. "There are a few over your left eye and at the back of your head, but that hardly equates to 'everywhere.' Look at it this way, you were too darned handsome for your own good anyway."

Ben had to remind himself that grown men didn't pout. "You used to say I looked noble."

"Well, what did you expect? That sandy blond hair and those smooth-planed features were the first things I saw when you took the bandages off my eyes. You might as well have been on a white charger as far as I was concerned." When he failed to respond to that, Jessie cleared her throat and tried again. "You know the swelling will go down, Doc, and the bruises will heal. I've had a look at your charts. Besides the broken collarbone and ribs, the worst injury seems to be that blow you took on the back of your head."

"Wrong. The worst injury is that I can't *see,*" Ben snapped, pointing at his eyes.

"But the doctors are sure your condition is only temporary. Your vision should return as soon as the swelling goes down."

"Spare me. I know the odds of these kinds of injuries healing, and sixty/forty isn't good enough."

Jessie remained silent for several seconds. Then Ben heard her adjust his untouched breakfast tray. "Well, you're definitely not going to get any better if your appetite doesn't improve."

"I'm not hungry."

"I thought you were concerned about your appearance? No one's going to call that five-foot-eleven-inch frame wiry if you skip any more meals. More than likely they'll strap you to the bed and force-feed you. Here," she said. Ben heard her shift dishes and cutlery. "We can talk while you're eating. The coffee's already getting cold. You'll find the handle at nine o'clock."

"I don't want any coffee."

"Uh-huh. Some people will do anything to get out of using a bedpan." She sat down on the side of the bed. "Mind if I have a piece of your toast? I didn't have time for breakfast this morning."

Before he could recover from the feel of her thigh pressing against his, Ben heard her spreading something on the bread, then taking a bite and chewing. It was so typical of her that he had to make a conscious effort not to smile. He had less luck in keeping his mouth from watering when he heard her low moan of pleasure.

"The peach preserve they gave you must be something they save for VIPs. We never get anything this good down at the cafeteria. Can't complain about the desserts, though. Yesterday they had double-fudge cake, you know the kind with the shavings of chocolate on top? I love the way those melt in my mouth."

Ben swallowed and tried to ignore that his stomach was pulling with hunger. But it seemed determined to notice every sound Jessie made. At its first embarrassing growl, he sought and found the mug and lifted it to his lips. Maybe a sip or two of coffee was all he needed to quiet the beast.

"How's your work going?" he asked, reluctantly. He didn't really want to get involved in a conversation, but he was hoping that if she was talking she'd have less time to eat. For all he cared she could have his breakfast; however, the least she could do was take it outside. "Are you still glad you decided to become a nurse?"

"Next to ignoring Aunt Evelyn's pessimistic outlook about my chances of having a double cornea transplant and seeing again, it's the best thing that has ever happened to me. There isn't a day that goes by that I don't get a new perspective of how much a nurse's emotional support can mean during a patient's convalescence. Besides," she added cheerfully, "where else can you bully someone into doing something and not get into trouble for it?"

For a moment Ben's expression grew tender. "Jessie, you never bullied anyone in your life—you never had to. You're far too clever in using charm and reverse psychology."

"Would you mind telling that to Mr. Purvis in Room 216? He's taken to calling me Holland the Hun. Oh, look at that bacon they gave you. Mr. Purvis loves bacon, but it's off his menu because his cholesterol level's too high. Mind if I have a piece? I promise to share."

Just as he caught on to her plan, she popped a portion of crispy bacon into his mouth. It was treachery at its lowest. The flavor ignited his taste buds and instead of protesting, he found himself chewing ravenously. "Damn you for a sneak, Jessie."

Her soft laugh reverberated with mischief. "There's no way you're going to be able to stop with one bite, either," she told him. Next thing he knew, she was trying to put a piece of toast wrapped around what he guessed was bacon into his hand. Naturally he resisted. "Sure, go ahead and make a mess," she said matter-of-factly. "But I'd better warn you that it'll be me stripping you out of this bed and those pajamas to clean up the crumbs."

That made Ben pause. It was the last thing he wanted—and not because he was a prude. He was no more prudish than the next man when faced with the prospect of being naked around a twenty-six-year-old, even if she was a nurse. But Jessie wasn't just any nurse, she was the young woman who three years ago had flung her arms around his neck and told him that she loved him.

"Don't flirt with me, Jessie," he said tightly.

"Don't flatter yourself, Dr. Collier," she shot back, though her voice sounded strained to Ben's ears. "If you must know, I bet Dr. Tremaine five dollars that I could stay in here more than ten minutes, and I'll win double that if I can get you to eat something."

"Well, it's not as if you can't afford the loss," Ben replied, beginning to feel even more testy. "Between your nurse's salary and your inheritance from your aunt, you're not exactly living on welfare."

"Hmph . . . and you were worried that I wasn't over my girlish crush on you? Here's a news flash, Doc. For all your good looks, I saw the light when I realized you have the romantic instincts of a squash."

Stunned, Ben could think of nothing to do but take a bite of his toast and bacon. As he chewed, he considered this new revelation.

She was over him. It was what he wanted, of course; after all, hadn't he gently but firmly pointed out that even if he was interested in becoming involved with someone, it would be someone more appropriate? She was twelve years his junior, for heaven's sake. Far too young for him.

Still...*over him*...that was a surprise, and it hardly seemed in keeping with the young woman he thought he knew.

Jessie, as she'd often liked to point out despite Ben's insistence that he didn't put much stock in astrology, was a Taurus. She'd explained that meant determination was her middle name. He'd eventually discovered it was true, though at times like this he was tempted to call it stubbornness. She also possessed an incomparable supply of patience, which was why Ben couldn't help being suspicious.

If Jessie had decided she was in love with someone, that was it. Earthquakes could chip away at continents and glaciers could cover what was left; her devotion would remain.

Taking another bite of his food, he chewed thoughtfully. "Jessie, dear," he said after swallowing, "I'm afraid I don't believe you."

"A squash," she insisted. "And believe me, I'm being generous."

She'd obviously misunderstood him. "Forget the squash. What I mean is that I didn't believe you when you said you're over me."

"Is that so?" The thrum of her fingers had Ben almost smiling. "You know, if I wasn't so worried about you, I'd consider leaving that mess on the wall for someone else to find. Of all the pompous things I've ever heard you say... I was right to see my mistake in falling for a Virgo. If it isn't habitual crankiness you people are renowned for, there's that streak of vanity to contend with."

"Now, Jessie, there's no need—"

"Say, speaking of romance, you know what?" she said abruptly, giving him no opportunity to finish. "I think Nurse Hodges has a crush on Calvin Shipley, our day-shift security guard. It's nothing I can put my finger on, but—"

Ben cautiously reached toward her voice and cupped his hand around her face. After stroking her cheek affectionately with his thumb, he gently pressed it against her lips. "I've embarrassed you, and that's the last thing I meant to do. But, my dear, you have to admit that we've been through a great deal together and, as a result, I have come to know you pretty well."

Jessie took hold of his wrist and removed his hand. "You *knew* a twenty-three-year-old innocent who with the aid of a walking stick and a little chutzpah blindly stumbled into your office in search of miracles. The first man I saw when I regained my sight was the man who gave it back to me. I know now that's why I thought I'd fallen in love with you. But I've done a lot of growing up since then. I— I've learned the difference between love and gratitude.''

How he wished he could believe that, because the truth was he'd missed her. The year that Jessie came into his life, he'd laughed more, felt more...oddly enough *seen* more. She possessed a talent to make people become aware of things outside their immediate existence, and he'd been pleased when he'd learned she'd chosen to seek her nursing degree in order to share that gift with people who needed her compassion and vitality. If he could be certain there wasn't a threat of hurting her again, he would like the chance to visit with her more often than those brief exchanges in the halls he'd resigned himself to before this happened to him. Talk friend to friend. Especially now. If anyone understood what he was going through, Jessica Holland did; she could appreciate the fear, the panic that was threatening to overcome him, the debilitating feeling of being totally isolated.

''Most of all I think I owe you a big hug for pointing out the difference between friendship and sexual attraction.''

About to reach for his coffee mug again, Ben froze. ''I beg your pardon?''

''Attraction...chemistry...you know.''

''Yes, I know about chemistry, but what does that have to do with— Wait a minute. Are you trying to say that you've become romantically involved with someone?''

''Have I ever,'' she gushed. She leaned closer to dab a napkin against the corner of his mouth and once again her scent flirted with Ben's senses. "Doc, can you keep a secret?"

"I always considered us friends, Jessie. Nothing has changed in that respect, and friends keep each other's secrets."

"Well, I don't know how to say this delicately, so I'll just tell you. I've met Mr. Right. The real one this time."

"Have you?" He thought it was going to take manual assistance to force his lips into a faint smile. Four little words and suddenly he felt very tired and very old. "I'm glad."

"I can't tell you what it means to hear you say that. And I think you'll approve of him because as you suggested, I did look for someone who was closer to my age this time. Doc, he's the sexiest thing since Jockey shorts, and it doesn't hurt that he makes me laugh more than anyone I've ever met."

"Sounds like a regular Adonis," Ben muttered under his breath.

"Excuse me?"

"I said, who is this personification of male perfection?"

"Who—uh—oh, dear. I'm not sure I can say, not even to you. You see, we're—we're trying to keep this as quiet as possible. Yes, that's exactly what we're doing, because as you well know, the hospital administration doesn't really like staff to get involved with each other on a personal basis."

"You mean your—" there was no way he could bring himself to use the term lover "—your friend works at the hospital?" It meant he probably knew the person, and somehow that only made Ben feel worse. "Now I am intrigued. Who is he, Jessie?"

"Marco."

"Marco!" The remnants of Ben's sandwich disintegrated in his crushing grip. "You can't be serious. You said he was someone closer to your own age. He's only two years younger than I am!"

"Chronologically maybe, but he's—he's young at heart."

"He *has* no heart, at least not where women are concerned. He's said that much himself. He's a wolf in playboy's clothing."

"I know about his reputation and we've talked about his past, but he insists that since I've come into his life, he's not interested in playing the field the way he used to."

"And how long have you been 'in his life'? I seem to recall that just before I—before this happened he was in hot pursuit of someone called Didi or Gigi who plays at a piano bar down on the River Walk."

"Okay, okay. Maybe it's only been about ten days. But, Doc, surely you can appreciate that sometimes these things happen quickly. Here. Drink some of your juice. All this talking seems to be making your throat scratchy."

Ben took the glass she placed in his hands, but only because he needed a moment to recover from shock. Marco Tremaine and Jessie? He sipped the juice and tried to come to terms with the idea. What he quickly discovered was that it was going to be difficult if not outright impossible.

He liked Marco; they were on friendly terms. But most of all he admired the ruggedly handsome doctor of Irish and Italian descent for being one of the best neurosurgeons in San Antonio. Common sense told Ben it would only have been a matter of time before Marco noticed Jessie because she was sweet and sincere and she had a natural type of prettiness that didn't require paint and sequins to attract attention. However, what troubled him was knowing that Marco seemed to possess one of the most cavalier attitudes toward women. How could he make Jessie see that without hurting her feelings or worse yet, sounding jealous?

He finished off his juice and carefully put down the glass. "Jessie. Damn, how am I going to say this and not— Do you trust me?"

"Now, Doc," Jessie scolded him with gentle rebuke. "What a question to ask someone who once put her future, correction, her life in your hands?"

Ben considered that and took what reassurance he could from it. "Then I'm going to ask you to do me a favor. I'm going to ask you to hold off becoming too intimately involved with Marco too quickly. Will you do that for me? I know you're all grown-up and that many girls—I mean women—your age are already married and have started families, but you're still so new at this man and woman business."

"Why, Doc, if I didn't know any better, I'd swear you cared."

"Of course I care!" Calm down, he admonished himself. He didn't want her thinking he was overly disturbed about this. Dignity, that's what the situation called for, dignity and restraint. "You're like—well, you're like a second sister to me."

"Gee. I don't know what to say."

Her voice was hushed, even hesitant. Good, Ben thought, she was touched. He'd been right to guess it wouldn't be wise to protest too strongly. More than likely gentle persuasion would make her see reason.

"You needn't say anything, don't you know that? It's like this visit— I didn't think I wanted company and now you've shown me how glad I am that you came by to check on me. Maybe you'll do it again? Keep me company and fill me in on what's going on around the place?" He reminded himself that in a way—as her doctor—he was the closest thing to family she had left. All right, maybe that was stretching things somewhat, but it wasn't too farfetched to pattern himself as a guardian of sorts, a benevolent friend directing her toward someone more—no, never mind that. What was important right now was getting her away from Marco. He would also have a long talk with Tremaine. The man wasn't unreasonable.

"What do you say, Jessie?" Though it hurt his lips, he twisted his mouth into a more engaging, though awkward smile. She'd once told him that he could make hearts flip-flop if only he would smile occasionally.

"Sure," she said, taking another piece of bacon and slapping it against a slice of toast. "For an *old* friend, I'd do just about anything. Now why don't you take a few more bites of this breakfast while I try to clean off that wall. I wouldn't want your reputation as our resident saint to be tarnished."

"You always were a kidder," Ben said, concentrating on keeping relief and satisfaction out of his voice. "I hope you realize that I wouldn't have done it if I'd known you were the one who was going to have to clean it up?"

"Be still my heart."

She'd risen from the bed and was crossing the room. Ben frowned. "I'm sorry. I didn't catch that."

"You weren't supposed to," she replied, as she picked up the broken bowl. "I was just counting my blessings."

Chapter Two

Jessica had been eleven when her father died. Shortly afterward, her mother came to the conclusion that it would be impossible for them to make ends meet on their own and moved them in with her father's older sister. Aunt Evelyn was a severe, pinched-mouth woman—a career widow, as Jessica came to think of her—who greeted Jessica into her home with a quote about nothing needing a lie and how faults that needed them most grew two as a result. Never mind that Jessica didn't tell lies—a small fib occasionally when she thought the truth might hurt someone she cared about—but certainly no outright lies. However, the humorless woman was convinced all children were masters of the art and as a result lectured incessantly about the nether world that would be their just reward.

Now as Jessica exited Ben's room and quietly drew the door closed behind her, the old saying came back to haunt her like a bad dream. Aunt Evelyn's headstone was probably doing a jig at this very moment because she'd finally done it. She'd told a lie—no way this could be watered down to a fib—and now she had double problems to contend with. Worst of all, it was no less than what she deserved.

She closed her eyes and drew in a deep breath. She needed a chance to stem another rush of tears; they seemed to want to flow at the most inopportune times these days. Since last Friday to be exact.

It had started the moment the news about Ben reached her via the hospital's supersonic gossip line. If she lived to be a hundred she knew she would never forget how she'd felt, since the experience was highlighted by her dropping a tray of medication in front of the head nurse. After hastily cleaning up the disaster and finding someone to cover for her, she'd raced to Emergency.

Of course that proved to be a waste of time. She hadn't been allowed to see him because she wasn't immediate family. She wasn't family at all, merely a previous patient; one of his success stories, true, but it wasn't as if there weren't a number of those. Within hours after the incident was reported on the news, phone calls, flowers and cards started pouring in from former and present patients, friends and colleagues. It proved that Ben was practically revered as a professional and as a man.

And minutes ago he told her that above all his patients, she'd been his favorite. He didn't need to know that she would cherish the admission until the day she died and that she was inanely tempted to go up to the roof and announce it to the population of greater San Antonio, just as he didn't need to be burdened with the knowledge that nothing had changed regarding her feelings for him. He needed to focus his energies on more pressing matters.

How it had broken her heart to see him lying there staring through her with those empty gray eyes. He'd always been such a dedicated doctor. Dynamic, but in a quiet, steady way. The man in the room behind her was a shell of his former self.

No wonder Marco had cornered her and cajoled, bullied and finally begged her for help. Someone needed to convince Ben to stop resisting the staff's efforts, stop resisting their prognosis for his recovery, and lift him out of his depressed state. Since Marco had witnessed her white-faced arrival in Emergency and had later dragged a confession from her regarding her feelings for Ben, he'd decided that maybe she was the one for the job.

"Get him to start focusing outward again," Marco said. "He needn't know your actions are based on anything more than the compassion you'd show another patient."

She'd warned him that Ben was sharper than that, explaining that he would see right through her, and she'd been right. How long had it been before Ben told her he didn't believe her flimsy reasons for coming to see him? Small surprise that she'd panicked.

What choice had she had but to react the way she did? She couldn't let him send her away, any more than she could allow him to give up on himself. Maybe she wasn't ready to confess as much to Marco, but given the chance she *knew* she could help Ben. If she could show him the worth of the world, the joy in living through her eyes, he would find hope—or at least the will to make the most of whatever options there were left open to him. No one knew better than she did how a positive mental attitude counted in these matters.

Then . . . perhaps . . . well, who could tell? Maybe if Ben gave her half a chance, maybe he would change his mind about her, about *them*. Maybe he could learn to care for her, not just as a friend, but in the same way she loved him.

A fine mess her good intentions had created, though. As Marco had requested, she'd given it her best shot, all right, but in the process she told her second lie. No way she was going to be able to pull off this scheme. Her and her big mouth. Granted, she'd been relieved when Ben swallowed that impulsive bit of fabrication about her and Marco. But what was Marco going to say after hearing what she'd gotten him into?

"Damn. Don't tell me it didn't go well?"

Jessica opened her eyes and found the object of her next immediate worry standing directly in front of her. Like her, he had dark, thick hair that had a tendency to curl so that it resembled black licks of wild flames. But that's where any resemblance between her and Dr. Marco Tremaine stopped.

An inch or two taller than Ben, Marco was a solidly built man whose finely honed muscles made him look like a body builder, but he was one of the hospital's most respected neurosurgeons. He was also undeniably handsome and, as she considered his dramatic, sharp features, she decided that unlike her, brooding was becoming to him. It gave his wide mouth a sexy something and his hooded eyes an even more intense quality. She could appreciate why women had a tendency to twitter like excited hens whenever he passed in his usual long-legged lope. He was a physiological dream. A woman would have to be in a mental fog to remain indifferent to him—or already crazy about someone else.

"Go well? That depends how you look at it," she said weakly. Then she gestured down the hall. "Could we move over there? I think he's developing bionic hearing."

They stopped in front of a supply room door. "All right, stop keeping me in suspense," Marco said, his already low voice deepening with growing concern. "Did you or didn't you get him to eat something?"

"Eat . . . sure, a little."

Relief replaced the tension in Marco's face. "Way to go! Hey, everybody— Jessie got Ben to eat!"

As the dozen or so staff members up and down the hallway gave either thumbs-up signals or low-key cheers, Jessica pressed back against the wall as if she'd been fingered in a police lineup. "Marco, I *really* need to talk to you about this."

"Go ahead, but can you make it quick? I'm due down in X-ray."

"In that case I can wait." Like for her next life when she came back as a toad. Wasn't progression or retrogression to various life-forms—depending on the success of one's preceding performance on earth—a principle of reincarnation? Jessica thought, remembering a college philosophy class. Either way, she was in trouble, she assured herself, inching away from the hand that was resting six inches from her head; the hand attached to the arm that blocked her in on one side.

Without so much as a blink, Marco raised his other arm, corraling her, then gently pushed her back in front of him with his clipboard. "Not so fast," he drawled, eyeing her with growing suspicion. "You're beginning to look like the scared mouse who used to share my efficiency apartment with me and my cat, Terminator. Now what haven't you told me? Were you being less than truthful when you said you got our friend to take some food?"

"Of course not, but...Marco, it wasn't exactly easy."

"I don't imagine it was. Why do you think I asked for your help?" His expression grew whimsical. "What happened, did he ask you to spoon out the pulp from his orange juice? Cut the crust off his toast? Heck, I know Ben can be something of a nit-picker at the best of times, but don't be too hard on him, Jessie."

"Marco—"

"More than likely hearing the dulcet tones of that sweet voice of yours reminded the man of that extra, wily Y chromosome he can't do anything with unless he gets well, and because it was *you* it affected him twice as much."

"Marco—"

"Honey, give yourself a break. Anyway, it's about time the guy woke up to the fact that he's human."

Ordinarily Jessica found Marco's grins contagious, but at the moment, she was more tempted to grab his view-blocking shoulders and shake him. "It wasn't anything like that. Ben behaved like a perfect gentleman, and I was happy to do what I could for him. But... remember what I told you about my history with him? Not that we really have what you'd call a history," she said quickly.

"Somebody throw me a life preserver," Marco groaned. "Jessie, we've waded through all this before. What's your point?"

"I'm trying to tell you. Remember when I said he'd never believe I was around only because I was doing Nurse Hodges a favor?"

"You're saying he saw through the ploy? Well, okay. So what? It turned out fine anyway, didn't it?"

"That depends on how you look at it."

"Then *how* exactly should I look at it?"

"I had to lie to him."

"Poor baby."

"This is serious, Marco. I had to make him believe, er, certain things."

"Whatever works, *cara mia*," he teased, wiggling his eyebrows at her.

Jessica decided the eyebrows had been inherited from the Latin side of his family and that right now only the Latin side of his brain was functioning. "I hope you feel the same way when I tell you what I had to resort to. It could result in a certain cramping of your usual style, Dr. Tremaine.''

''*My* style?''

Finally, she had his complete attention . . . the Irish grim poets' side. In fact, right now the look on his face wasn't unlike Aunt Evelyn's habitual scowl.

''I had to convince Ben that I was over my so-called crush on him,'' she said, trying to break her news gently.

''Aha. I think I'm beginning to figure out what you're driving at.''

As Jessica saw the twinkle returning to his eyes, she knew he'd not only figured out what she'd been trying to tell him but in typical Tremaine fashion he was expanding on the premise. There were probably, she decided with an inner sigh, easier ways to make a living and still serve mankind. Maybe she should look into selling time-share resort condominiums. Maybe she could inquire about that Help Wanted sign in the window of the doughnut shop across the street from the hospital.

''Try not to look as though you've just been invited to raid the refrigerator at a four-star trattoria,'' she said dryly. ''It was a decision made in a moment of panic. I'm no more interested in you than you're interested in me.''

''Mmm . . . it would make me feel like I was dating my kid sister. In fact, if it wasn't for this little guy,'' he drawled, running his finger down her upturned nose, ''and those *Jane Eyre* eyes, you could be.''

But there was still a trace of flirtation in his dark gaze and shaking her head Jessica swatted away his hand. "Marco, will you give it a rest and listen to what I'm trying to tell you."

"I'm listening. You had to convince our mutual friend you were no longer pining away for him."

"I never said anything about pining. I said—okay, you're right, I had to convince him. There didn't seem to be any choice. So I told him I was interested in you."

"Don't beat yourself up about it," Marco said, giving her a gentle cuff under her chin. "You chose the most believable candidate."

"Oh, brother."

"What did I say? It's the truth. Should I go shave my head and whip myself on the back with my stethoscope because women find me attractive?"

"I told Ben that the attraction was mutual," she muttered. "In fact more than mutual. I let him think you'd never met anyone like me before." For a small eternity Marco simply stared at her, until Jessica gave him a poke in the vicinity of his navel. "Stop that! If you're going to get angry, go ahead and do it. Only remember that *you're* the one who drafted me to work on him."

"I'm not angry. I just need a minute to get used to the idea."

"Can you do it without that suffering look on your face?"

"I'm Irish-Italian, not Greek-Russian. I can do maybe ten seconds of 'suffering,' but then we have to break out the Chianti." Shrugging, he reached out to toy with a strand of her hair. "Okay, kiddo, so we supposedly have a mutual admiration society going.

Exactly how interested did you say you and I were with each other?''

"How's the word 'crazy' sit with you? And, um, I also mentioned something about you being the greatest thing since Jockey shorts.'' She would have thought that it was impossible for Marco Tremaine to blush, but twin spots of color appeared at his cheeks. She grasped the hand he'd dropped onto her shoulder and patted it reassuringly. ''Don't worry. I don't expect you to live up to the reputation.''

"Are you crazy?'' he wheezed. Belatedly he glanced around. ''Geez, Jessie. He's going to think that we're actually... you know.''

"Don't remind me. Look, I'm sorry for putting you on the spot, but I couldn't think of anyone who has a worse reputation than you do.''

"Oh, thanks.''

"I only meant with women.''

"Why don't you stop before you hit an artesian well in China. No wonder you haven't gotten anywhere with Collier.'' Seeing her wounded look he sighed and shifted to smooth the hair at his nape. ''Sorry. Forget my macho posturing. It's just that I don't see myself as being quite the hedonist you make me out to be. I may date a lot of women, but they always know the score from the beginning, know what I mean?''

"Sure,'' Jessica murmured, ducking her head and concentrating on her neatly laced nurse's shoes. ''Anyway, I was the one being rude.''

"Nah.'' Marco adjusted his tie. ''Okay, feed me my lines. Where do you want me to take it from here?''

"What I'd like is for you to stay away from him.''

"No can do. I'm the neurologist on the case, remember?"

And Ben needed the best. Jessica should have known better than to ask him to replace himself. But she couldn't help worrying about how he was going to treat Marco now that he knew—or thought he knew—about their relationship.

"In that case I don't have the vaguest idea," she replied honestly.

Marco tugged at his earlobe. "Hmm... I take it that he doesn't approve of the idea of you and me?"

"I think what bothers him the most is that he likes you," Jessica said, trying to make up for some of her previous bluntness.

"Alas, he likes *you* better."

Jessica lowered her gaze again. "It must be some latent protective instinct, that's all. What with my mother passing away just after I graduated from college and my aunt last year, he probably feels sorry for me."

"Maybe, but some of the world's greatest romances have started on less substance." At Jessica's wary look, Marco raised his empty hand and the clipboard in surrender. "Don't start protesting. It was merely a rhetorical observation."

"It doesn't matter if I did have more feelings for him than were healthy. What's important right now is turning around his mental state, just as you said."

Marco placed his hand under her chin and lifted it. "Go tell that to that custodian's wash bucket down the hall, Miss Heart-On-Her-Sleeve. You're hooked on the guy. What harm will it do if we concentrate on getting us *both* what we want?''

"Why do I get the feeling there's a subtle shift of control going on here?'' Jessica muttered, not at all sure she liked it. "And since when did you become an advocate of the Happily Ever After Club?''

"There you go again, insinuating I have a gilded heart. Listen, my parents have been married for forty years and produced eight *bambini*. Someday I want the same thing for myself.''

With a lift of her left eyebrow, Jessica drawled, "Really. So what are you waiting for?''

"I'm not ready yet. Sir Ben the Bashful on the other hand is another matter entirely.'' Marco glanced at his watch and groaned. "Enough. If feeding our mutual friend a line is what it's going to take, then we'll do it. You and I are now the Romeo and Juliet of San Antonio General . . . the Mark Antony and Cleopatra . . . the F. Scott and Zelda.''

"Marco, all those relationships ended in tragedy,'' Jessica intoned.

"This isn't going to work if you're going to think literally. Never mind. We need to table this until later anyway. Why don't you give me a quick kiss so I can get down to X-ray before they start paging me.''

The casually spoken suggestion had Jessica staring at him open-mouthed. "I will not!''

Marco leaned over and whispered, "You will so. We're supposed to be nuts about each other, remember?''

"But people are watching.''

Lifting his eyes to the ceiling, Marco mumbled something in Italian. "That's the whole idea, my little airhead. The faster the viperous tongues of gossip begin twaddling, the faster Ben will get confirmation of your story and the sooner he'll start warning me off. When that doesn't work, he'll get agitated. *That* will get his mind off himself and his problem and, before you know it, we should see signs of improvement in his condition. Now lay one on me, right here," he said, pointing to his puckered lips.

Instead Jessica glanced around, wondering why there seemed to be twice as many people in the hallway as before. "Marco—can't we take things a bit slower? Me kissing you in the middle of this wing isn't exactly going to do my reputation wonders."

With a sigh of exasperation, Marco straightened. "You're right, what could I have been thinking. It's my job to do the kissing," he said a moment before ducking his head and planting a solid smack on her lips.

Jessica didn't have time to protest. Before she knew it the kiss was over and someone down the hall was wolf-whistling at them. "Have you lost your mind?" she whispered, reaching up to see if her nurse's cap was still on her head. "Employees are not supposed to be seen fraternizing while on duty."

"Well, what good would it do if I dragged you into the supply closet? Besides, we weren't fraternizing, we were kissing."

"For which we both could be fired or at the least receive a severe reprimand!"

"Don't worry. The head honchos are always the last to hear about these things. I'll talk to you later after I check in on our friend and find out how he reacts to me. *Ciao,* kiddo. Hold that elevator," he called rushing down the hall.

"Marco!" He spun around, the tails of his long lab coat swinging and giving him an added aura of dash that he hardly needed. "Lipstick," she mouthed, pointing to her lips.

He rubbed at his mouth and saw the pink gloss. Grinning, he reached into his pocket for a handkerchief. With a wink and a wave he disappeared into an elevator.

Wanting nothing less than to blend in with the anemic beige wall, Jessica groaned. Great, she thought, Cinderella got a fairy godmother and who did she get stuck with? A half-Irish, half-Italian fruitcake. Why couldn't she have settled for going down to the church on the corner and lighting a few candles as she always did for patients who could use an extra word put in for them upstairs? She wasn't Catholic, but she'd long ago decided the technicality didn't matter.

"Holding up the wall, nurse?"

The chilly voice of the floor supervisor jarred Jessica out of her trance. Straightening, she gave her a weak smile. "No, ma'am. Excuse me."

Avoiding the other woman's eyes, she hurried down the hallway asking herself if maybe, just maybe, she hadn't let herself in for more trouble than she could handle.

Chapter Three

When the door to his room swung open, Ben turned his head toward the sound, trying not to look too expectant. It was damned hard. Now that Jessie had breached his defensive armor, there was little else to do to pass the interminable hours except to wait for her—and it was driving him crazy.

"Good morning, Dr. Collier."

It wasn't Jessie; it was one of the other nurses. Disappointment was like a plunging elevator leaving behind an empty shaft deep inside him. Ben didn't bother attempting to place a face with the voice, as the psychiatrist who'd visited had suggested he try to do to entertain himself. His spirits, hardly euphoric to begin with, settled once again in a pit of apathy.

"What's so good about it?"

"Why it's the Fourth of July. And what a wonderful day it's promising to be, too. The sky is clear and the birds are singing especially nice this morning. Would you like me to open this window while it's still pleasant so we can hear?"

"Aren't you worried that I might be tempted to jump out?"

The nurse's lusty burst of laughter had him wondering if he didn't belong on stage at one of those comedy nightclubs. "I'd think twice about it if I were you. Remember, we're only two floors up. Those oleander shrubs below your window would likely slow your fall and you'd probably only break a leg or two. Then again you could knock out the window in the process and cut yourself. But I doubt you'd bleed to death before someone found you."

Good grief, Ben thought bringing his teeth together with a snap, no wonder she'd been amused at his acerbic remark. The woman was a fan of comedy all right—black comedy. And he'd believed Nurse Hodges was bad. What was going on around here?

In the two days since Jessie first visited him, something had happened. He was no longer being treated with the sympathy and respect that he had been. Gone was any trace of the compassion that had underscored everyone's attitude when they came into his room. Not that he needed or wanted anyone's pity; but the 180-degree turn was grating on the nerves nevertheless. He deserved better treatment—if for no other reason than because he was a paying patient! Was everyone going off the deep end? What else could it be, since he knew *he* wasn't the one losing his mind. In fact, if he hadn't been the logical, practical person he was, he would have begun to suspect Jessie of having something to do with all of this.

However, he *did* know better. Jessie could be impulsive, even mischievous, but there wasn't a conniving bone in her body. No way anyone would convince him that she'd talked his attending physicians and nurses into ignoring his silences and to stop placating his depression. Someone with more clout than she possessed had authorized such a group effort, and he didn't have to think hard to guess who that person had been.

Returning his attention to his current intruder, he listened as she opened the window. Along with the mild breeze that filled the room and teased his senses, he caught the scent of rosewater. Now he recognized who was she was: Nurse Scott, a short, pear-shaped woman whose tightly permed hair reminded him of a steel wool pad.

"Where's Nurse Holland?" he demanded, deciding he was going to enlighten Jessie of Marco's little stratagem.

"I haven't seen her in a while. Why? Are you expecting her?"

The woman was sharp. No doubt she would report everything he said to Marco the moment she left him. "Not really. But she did say she was going to read me the newspaper this morning."

"That's real thoughtful of her, I'm sure. But don't forget she has other patients to attend to who need her for more important things than to entertain them. Of course, she may be taking an early break. Come to think of it, Dr. Tremaine hasn't been around for the last few minutes either, so you know what that could mean.'' Another chuckle, this one a painful imitation of a schoolgirl's titter, filled the room. "My...it makes a person feel good to see young love, and what a handsome couple they make.''

Ben scowled. He could have gone all day without hearing *that*. "I hadn't noticed.''

"Oh, indeed. They've been the talk of the hospital ever since he kissed her right out here in the hallway. There now,'' she said, brushing her hands together as she approached the bed. "Do we need assistance getting to the bathroom, Doctor?''

"No, *we* do not,'' Ben muttered, still thinking about what he'd just heard. He found it was too easy to picture Jessie in Marco's arms and he didn't like it one bit. Not because he was jealous, he quickly assured himself, but because she should know better than to show such blatant disregard for hospital regulations. So should Marco.

Is that any reason to take your foul mood out on the messenger? You're in no position to figure out when or how she might seek revenge.

Realizing he'd made a critical mistake and that Nurse Scott's silence probably meant she was staring holes into him, Ben sighed. "What I mean to say is that I've already managed that impressive feat on my own. But thank you,'' he added as an afterthought.

"Excellent, Doctor. Self-motivation is the seed from which recuperation will flourish. If you'll excuse me for one teensy moment, I'll bring in our breakfast.

Nurse Hodges will be by later and we'll have a nice shave."

"You two go ahead and indulge without me." Ben decided he was in no mood for playing the diplomat. There was, after all, a limit to everything. He was getting fed up with listening to her singsong voice and he was definitely tired of that universal "we" nonsense. "I don't want to be shaved, especially not by that butcher. My face is still sore from yesterday's carving job."

"I'm sure you're exaggerating."

"Think so? Hang around and see for yourself—if you have the stomach for it."

"Shame on you, Doctor. You know perfectly well that Gloria Hodges is considered one of the most conscientious and gentle nurses at this hospital," she told him sternly. "Now behave while I go get that tray."

The last of Ben's tolerance was engulfed by flaming indignation. "I don't want any damned breakfast. For that matter I never said I wanted my window open either! Can't you just go bother someone else?"

"Really, sir, I'm only trying to do my—"

"Out!"

The door to his room burst open. "My goodness, what's going on here?" Jessie demanded, rushing in.

Relief swept through Ben along with several other emotions, a few even disconcerting; however, it was residual feelings of hurt and abandonment that saved him from exhibiting anything but sarcasm. "Well, look who's come to join us. *We* didn't take you away from anything important, did we, Nurse Holland?

Never mind. Would you kindly inform this person that I do not wish to listen to a bunch of birds cackling, nor am I interested in ingesting tasteless, lukewarm calories. Furthermore, I have no intention of shaving again until I can do it myself!''

''I see there's no need to ask how he is this morning,'' Jessie drawled to the maligned nurse.

Before Ben could offer his own comment to that, Nurse Scott sniffed. ''All I wanted to do was freshen up the room and serve him his breakfast.''

Ben had no idea what happened next. He heard a brief fluttering sound and then Nurse Scott's titter. The door was opened and someone walked out, only to return a moment later.

''Thank you very much, dear,'' Nurse Scott said warmly. ''I can't tell you how much I appreciate this. I don't know what's come over the man.''

That had Ben stiffening with indignation anew. But when the door once again closed with a definitive thump, his frown of irritation turned to dismay. ''Jessie? Wait!''

Setting the tray on the bed table, Jessie asked, ''Wait for what? To be treated to the same charming manners you just subjected Bea to?''

''I thought you'd—uh . . .''

''Left?'' she said helpfully.

''Never mind,'' he mumbled, not quite ready to concede he'd behaved like a first-class louse.

''Splendid idea.'' She rolled the table up from the foot of the bed to where Ben could reach the tray. Then she poured coffee from the small glass coffee server and adjusted the mug so he would easily find it.

"Doc, you have to stop biting everyone's head off. You're ruining your sterling reputation."

"I wouldn't if everyone would leave me alone the way I'd asked them to. And look who's talking about ruined reputations," he added, unable to stop himself.

"What's that supposed to mean?"

"Exactly what it sounds like." Ben forgot everything else he'd been planning to say to her and focused on what disturbed him most. "I heard about you and Marco being caught in a compromising situation the other day."

"Compromising? Oh . . . that. It was only a kiss."

He couldn't believe she was being so casual about something that could have such serious repercussions. "People are talking about it all over the hospital, Jessie. It's a miracle Administration hasn't heard about it yet."

"I suppose you're right. Coffee mug at nine o'clock." As he reluctantly but obediently reached for it, she told him she was cutting the fresh cantaloupe decorating his oat bran waffle into bite-sized pieces. "I told Marco that I didn't think we should be open about our feelings, but he said he couldn't help himself."

Ben nearly bit off a mouthful of ceramic. Marco was worse than reckless, he was a fool with a short memory. The other day, after Jessie had confided her situation to Ben, he'd had a talk with the doctor and asked him to think twice before getting more deeply involved with her. Things had been sticky at first; Marco accused him of having ulterior motives, even going so far as to suggest Ben was harboring feelings for Jessie himself. Eventually, however, Ben convinced him that he was simply concerned about Jessie's reputation and her future at the hospital.

But apparently Marco had only been paying Ben lip service and had no intention of being any more discreet than he was with the other women he'd developed infatuations for and quickly tired of. It distressed Ben and he knew he couldn't let the situation continue. Yet what else could he do about it?

"Hey, are you falling asleep on me?" Jessica teased, easing the mug from his hands and setting it back on the tray.

"No . . . just thinking."

"That's obvious." She spread the napkin over his lap. "You're disappointed in me, aren't you?"

The sigh that preceded the question was as soft as her touch when she replaced the mug with a fork, and it caused an odd, aching sensation deep in Ben's chest. "I thought I was, but I'm discovering it's not that simple. You're a loving and giving person, Jessie. You can't be blamed for someone being attracted to you, for wanting to possess those qualities for himself."

"You're referring to Marco?"

"Of course I'm referring to Marco. Who else? Did he tell you about our talk?" Ben asked cautiously. At Jessie's equally careful confirmation, he grimaced. "Please don't be upset with me. I couldn't stand by and remain silent. You mean a great deal to me . . . too much not to ask him to be extra careful with you . . . with your vulnerability to him."

"I'm getting too old for fathering, Doc."

Is that how she saw this? Ben frowned as he located a piece of cantaloupe with his fork. Is that what he'd been reduced to in her eyes, a surrogate father figure? What happened to her romantic feelings for him? They couldn't have been extinguished that quickly. She might not have the wisest taste in men, but she wasn't fickle.

To his relief, she'd taken him up on his offer to visit him whenever she had some spare time. He might still be slightly miffed that she would choose to be with Marco first and foremost, but despite that hadn't he and Jessie grown closer again, regaining a rapport they hadn't shared in ages?

"You're not supposed to just hold that fork," she told him, breaking into his thoughts. "You're supposed to use it to eat, especially when you're lucky to be on a diet that's less restrictive than most patients'." After he ate the slice of fruit, she directed the fork to a piece of the waffle. "Watch out for the syrup or it'll—oops."

Before she could finish warning him, he'd lifted the waffle toward his mouth and a drop of the sticky condiment splattered on his chin. Jessica sat down on the bed and used an extra napkin to wipe it away—despite Ben's grumbling that he wasn't a child and could do it himself.

"I know you can. Keep eating."

He muttered again, but did as he was told, earning Jessica's soft-spoken approval. At first it was disgruntling to be hovered over; however, it wasn't long before he forgot about the indignity of being treated as if he were still in diapers and focused on the simple pleasure of having his friend near.

You mean having a woman near. Face it, Ben, old man, it's been a while since you felt a woman's thigh pressed against yours, with or without a sheet and clothing between you, and Jessie's the sweetest kind of temptation.

"You know for a blond-haired man, you certainly have a heavy beard."

Ben was grateful for the interruption of his wayward thoughts. "That's because it isn't the same color as my hair. I discovered that myself while in college during a summer break. A friend and I were biking to California and, being on shoestring budgets, bathroom facilities weren't always available. So I decided to abandon the idea of shaving every day. The beard grew out red. Between my sunburn, windburn and beard, I looked like a Viking with a devil of a hangover."

"You rode a bike to California? Isn't that something... I've never thought of you as being athletically inclined."

"Just because I don't have Marco's Neanderthal build—"

"I wasn't comparing."

Ben could hear the underlying hurt in her voice and immediately regretted his bristled response. With a muttered oath, he set down his fork on the plate, reached for and found her slender shoulder. "Ah, Jessie...you're trying so hard and I keep knocking you down, don't I?"

"At least you notice."

She sounded like a gloomy child who'd won the consolation prize in a mudpie contest. He lifted one corner of his mouth in a halfhearted attempt at a smile. "I notice."

"And just for the record, he doesn't have a Neanderthal build."

"Spoken like a woman who's looking through rose-tinted glasses."

"That's not very nice or fair."

"Fair! Do you have any idea of what he's up to? He has everyone on my case. If I don't eat, I get nagged. If I criticize a nurse's slow response to my page, I get nagged. If I refuse to do my therapy, I get nagged."

"Now you're exaggerating."

"Ha!"

"All right, maybe some of the staff are trying a different technique with you, but it's only because they care. We all care."

"*You* do," he agreed gruffly, his annoyance seeping away under her warm reassurance. But as he grew aware of a stronger temptation to do more than simply touch her shoulder, he abruptly withdrew his touch. "Damn," he muttered, mostly to himself. "It's probably nothing more than cabin fever getting the best of me."

Jessie was silent for a moment and then he felt her lay a comforting hand on the one balled into a fist on his thigh. "I can cure that. That is if you're willing to be open-minded and trust me?"

Startled, Ben jerked his head toward the sound of her voice. "What?"

"Some young musicians from one of the area's high schools are going to be playing down in the solarium today as a special Fourth of July treat. If you'd like, I could take you down there during my lunch break. I know it's not much, but it would give you a chance to get away from these four walls for a while."

Ben almost laughed. For a second he thought she was about to suggest something far more intimate; the not-so-funny thing was he didn't know whether he was relieved or disappointed.

"I don't think I'm in the mood to listen to John Philip Sousa, Jessie."

"They're not going to be playing marching music. These are members of the concert orchestra." Her tone was coaxing as she placed the fork back in his hand and directed him to another piece of cantaloupe. "The string section to be exact. I understand they're going to play mostly chamber music."

That was a different story, Ben thought, thinking of how he missed his own considerable CD collection of classical music at home. He often relaxed with a brandy and a violin sonata, particularly after a stressful day, and just as often because he simply had a craving for that type of music. But would Jessie like it? "You'd probably be bored," he murmured, knowing he couldn't enjoy himself if he thought she was making a sacrifice. "Young people don't go in for the classics these days. They like lots of percussion and steel guitar solos."

"Do they? I'm sorry to burst your bubble, oh wise one, but you're wrong, at least about me. When we first came to live with my aunt—before my eyesight began to deteriorate—she insisted I learn to play some kind of instrument and started me on violin lessons."

"I never knew that," Ben murmured, automatically turning his hand and taking possession of hers. He traced the shape and length of each finger. "Yes... I should have noticed them before. They're strong but elegant hands," he told her, while musing over their slightness compared to his. And had he ever really noticed how soft her skin was? Like doctors', nurses' hands were in water so often, yet Jessie's skin was remarkably smooth. "You would probably have become an accomplished violinist."

"Wrong again," Jessica replied, laughter in her voice. "It takes more than the right hands to play well, it takes a good ear. But as fate would have it, I turned out to be practically tone-deaf. Well, what do you say, do we have a date or not?"

A date. Those two words had a surprisingly strong impact on Ben. He told himself it was because it reminded him of his last outing, an arranged date with a divorceé he escorted to some event—a tedious experience since she hadn't had her legal separation long enough to speak of her ex-spouse without sarcasm.

But it wasn't the bitter brunette he pictured across from him at a candlelit table, it was Jessie... Jessie in a silvery-green, off-the-shoulder dress that made her eyes shimmer with secrets and promises and her bared skin glow like satin. Dragging his hand from hers, he pinched the bridge of his nose and squeezed his eyes shut.

"Doc? Are you all right?"

"Fine—um—it's not that I don't want to get out of this place, Jessie, but I'm not sure I'm up to actually mingling with the public yet. My face is still raw and swollen and—"

As he shifted his hand to his still bandaged head, Jessie drew it back down. "Stop that and listen to me. You're in a hospital, for heaven's sake. If you can't feel comfortable walking around here, where can you? Now, last chance...do you want me to come get you or should I invite one of my less trying patients?"

"I think I liked you better when you resorted to flattery to get your way," Ben muttered, frowning in her direction, even though it pulled at the stitches over his eye. But reminding himself that at least if she was with him, she couldn't be off someplace with Marco, he gave in. "All right, it's a date—on one condition," he added firmly. "That is if you grow bored, you'll be honest enough to tell me and bring me back here."

"Yes, Dr. Doom and Gloom."

Her voice was rich with amusement, and he thought the kiss she awarded his cheek made his nervous system send out enough voltage to kickstart a nuclear power plant. That made it all the more startling to feel her rise from the bed. "Where are you going?"

"I need to check on my other patients. You look like you can manage without me for a while."

"But you said you'd read me the paper."

"And I will. Give me ten minutes, fifteen tops and I'm all yours. *Ciao.*"

The door thumped closed behind her. *Ciao?* He'd been fine—wonderful until that. Nothing else she could have said would have burst Ben's bubble of contentment and quiet euphoria more abruptly.

What was he doing? He was supposed to be carefully, benevolently urging Jessica away from Marco, but not setting himself up as a replacement. Yet even as he told himself that, he knew all the denials and posturing in the world couldn't make him deny that when Jessie had kissed him, he'd wanted, hungered for more.

"*Ciao* indeed," he muttered.

"You don't have to go if you don't want to."

"I said I would go and I will."

"Would you like me to get you a wheelchair?"

"No. You're the one who said my leg muscles were going to atrophy if I didn't get out of this bed soon. Why bother getting out if you're going to stick me in a chair?"

Jessica watched Ben swing his legs over the side of the bed and slip his feet into his slippers. Now what? she wondered. A few hours ago everything had been fine between them. But even when she'd read him the paper, she'd noticed he'd withdrawn from her. Now his mood was almost as dark as it was at breakfast.

"I'm only trying to make this as pleasant an ordeal for you as possible, Doc. Now I'm holding your robe. If you'll stand, I'll help you slip into it," she said softly, clutching the navy-and-white striped garment that had been among the things his mother had brought from his condominium. When she felt him stiffen as she reached around him to tie the belt, she sighed and laid her cheek against his back. She heard his heartbeat accelerate; it was the only thing that gave her the courage to speak her mind. "Please . . . won't you tell me what I've done to upset you so I can apologize and we can be friends again?"

"You don't owe me any apology."

Jessica frowned, trying to analyze his tone as much as the words he spoke. The words came awkwardly, as if forced; on the other hand, the underlying emotion she recognized in his voice was—could she hope wistfulness?

"Well, I'm sorry anyway. I only tease you to try to get you out of your shell, Doc. You should know that. The last thing I'd ever want to do is hurt you."

"Jessie—" He sighed. "I know."

Why, she wondered, did he make it sound like a guilty verdict being handed down in a courtroom, when he'd more than once told her all they ever could be were friends? Before she could think of an answer, he turned around and looped an arm over her shoulders.

"Ignore me. Let's go."

She would have liked to pursue the matter—she hated things to be left dangling—but he was already reaching out with his right hand to find the door. Deciding she should be grateful that whatever the problem was, he seemed to have dealt with it in his own mind, she kept one arm around his waist and led him from the room.

The hallway was buzzing with normal activity. Jessica eased Ben around gurneys and slower pedestrian traffic. Whenever they approached doctors and nurses who knew him, they pantomimed their applause to

Jessica and called greetings to him. Though he returned their hellos amiably enough, his hold on her tightened.

"The worst of it's over. We're at the elevators," she told him soothingly and gave him a squeeze back. "You're doing great."

"I feel as if I'm on exhibition."

"Mmm." She couldn't resist a soft chuckle. "Every nurse we pass looks sorry you're no longer wearing one of those open-backed hospital gowns."

"That's *not* what I meant," he replied under his breath.

Grinning at his heightened color, she guided him into the elevator and pressed the first floor button. "I know it isn't, but I couldn't resist. Now try to relax," she added when he continued to stand rigidly. "We're alone in the car."

When the doors slid open again, they were immediately greeted by soft lilting strains of music. "Isn't it lovely?" Jessica said, this time taking Ben's hand to lead him out of the elevator and toward the solarium.

"Not bad. It's Haydn. I like Beethoven better."

"Why am I not surprised?"

"What do you mean?"

"He's wonderful, of course, but so brusque."

"And I am, too, I take it?"

Because he sounded sincerely wounded, Jessica didn't make light of the matter as she'd intended and, instead, sought to explain her remark. "Sometimes, yes. Maybe not brusque, exactly, but reserved, formal."

"You might as well come out and say it. You think I'm stuffy."

"But an endearing stuffy," she murmured.

She led him to a teal blue love seat by one of the ceiling to floor windows that looked out over the garden. When Ben remained silent, Jessica went on to describe the four young musicians sitting across the room and the number of patients and staff who were watching with rapt attention. She knew better than to push him anymore. If she knew one thing about Dr. Benedict Collier it was that he gave new meaning to the word reticent. When he had something to say, he'd let her know.

After a moment, as if she hadn't spoken, he said, "I don't mean to come off as stuffy."

Jessica laid her other hand over the one she still held and gazed at his profile. Bruised or not, he made her heart ache with love and yearning. "I know. I shouldn't have teased you, Ben, especially—" She'd almost said, especially when it was his solemnity and dedication that drew her in the first place.

"Especially what?"

"Especially when you know how much I admire your achievements, Doc," she said instead.

She watched him consider that and then relax, almost smile. "I don't mind you using my first name. You haven't in a long time. I didn't realize how much I'd missed it."

She could have hugged him. "It's not exactly appropriate for a nurse to call a doctor by his first name," she reminded him instead. But she knew the excuse was a weak one and that they both remembered the real reason; since that day in his office when he'd gently but firmly turned her away, she'd used the appellation to remind herself to keep an emotional distance.

"Maybe not, but it appears that no matter how much we try, we don't exactly have a normal doctor-nurse relationship, do we?" With a sad twist of his lips, he stretched his hand toward the warmth of the sun. "Why don't you tell me what it looks like out there? Last time I came by here only the Easter lilies were blooming."

Though she would have much preferred to pursue their present line of discussion, Jessica looked beyond the potted plants that filled the solarium, through the windows to the garden area that was closed in by a tall, wrought iron fence. The arched design gave the garden a Spanish aura, and the vines that climbed it offered both shade and a striking background for the more tender flowers inside the fenced area.

"The hibiscus are starting to look like man-eating plants," she said, leaning close so she wouldn't disturb those people nearby who were avidly listening to the musicians.

"Man-eating, eh? You needn't suppress that romantic streak for me, you know."

"Who's repressing? I'm serious. The blossoms are at least six inches wide and the new buds look like they're going to be even bigger."

"Are the orchids blooming yet?"

"There's a chartreuse yellow one just to the right of the fountain...oh, and there's a chameleon on the stem. He must have spotted something because he's filling his whatchamacallit and looks like he swallowed a cherry sourball."

Ben's eyes crinkled at the corners. "Cherry sourball . . . Jessie, you're still so young at heart."

"Well, what would you call it?"

"A red air sack, I suppose."

"Wow, why couldn't I think of that?" But Jessica almost sighed with contentment. This was exactly the kind of moment she dreamed of sharing with Ben—well, maybe she would have been open to something slightly more intimate. If only he would put his arm around her, lean close and kiss her. But considering the circumstances, she would happily take what she could get.

"I have a confession to make," Ben said after a few moments.

"What is it?"

"I'm having a nice time."

"Oh, Ben…I'm so glad," she whispered, her throat aching.

But no sooner did she turn back to the quartet than she spotted Marco coming down the hall. Nothing could have shattered her bubble of contentment faster.

"What's wrong?"

"Nothing."

"Don't 'nothing' me. You just went stiff. What's wrong?"

Jessica ignored him and focused her attention on the musicians hoping that Marco wouldn't spot them and come over. But out of the corner of her eye, she saw she wasn't going to be so lucky. She tried to signal him by shaking her head. The rascal ignored her.

"Hey, beautiful." His voice a sexy rumble, he swooped down behind them and nuzzled close to Jessie's ear. "Why is it that every time I turn around you're hanging around this guy?"

Though Jessica shifted enough to glare at him, she kept her tone pleasant. "Ben needs exercise so I talked him into coming down here to listen to the music with me."

"That's great . . . as long as he doesn't get any ideas about stealing my girl." Ignoring Jessie's mouthed entreaty that he leave, he added, "Listen, I'm glad I found you. Some old college friends are in town and I told them I'd join them for dinner. Want to come?"

"You know I have to work late tonight," she replied, speaking volumes with her eyes. "Besides, if they're school friends, I'm sure you'd have a better time reminiscing alone."

"Nah. Besides I told them all about you and they're dying to meet the woman who's managed to wrap me around her little finger."

Right now, Jessica thought, she could happily wrap her hands around his neck! "Marco, why don't we—"

"Er, Jessie, I don't mean to interrupt," Ben injected quietly, keeping his rigid-featured face turned toward the musicians. "But I think this is more tiring than I imagined it would be. Do you think you could find me a wheelchair and get me back to my room?"

Jessica caught Marco signaling her by touching his thumb and index finger together. She shook her fist at him in reply, then told Ben, "Of course. Stay here and I'll be right back with one."

As soon as she was out of earshot, Marco leaned down to whisper to Ben. "Nice try, but it won't work, buddy."

"I'm afraid I don't know what you're talking about."

"Of course you do, but have it your way. Only remember that you had your chance with her and now it's my turn."

He walked away and Ben remained sitting there, pretending to listen to the music. Inside, however, he was seething.

He resented Marco for trying to turn this into a contest. He resented the fact that Jessie couldn't see what Marco was doing. Most of all he hurt because he had a feeling he was realizing the truth too late. Was it possible that he'd let something, *someone*, very precious slip through his fingers?

Chapter Four

A week dragged by for Ben and then another. He kept track of the days according to which bandage came off when, which series of stitches were removed. Attending interns and nurses huddled like a Greek chorus insisting that he was looking better every day. They acted as if he should be throwing himself a party. No one seemed to notice that he didn't share their enthusiasm, and wouldn't—until he experienced some change in his vision.

The one bright spot through it all was Jessie. Sympathetic and supportive, she continued to spend every free minute with him that she could, reading him newspapers, business magazines or the messages on cards sent to his office that his staff forwarded. Every few days she dialed his parents' and sister's phone numbers, then thrust the phone into his hand coaxing him to let them know how he was doing. He grumbled about that, mostly because it made her laugh and he liked hearing the sound.

However, despite their increased time spent together, Ben had yet to get her to see that she and Marco weren't suited for each other. Invariably it was when Jessie was in his room that Marco came by to invite her out. Usually, Ben noted, it was on a day Marco should have known she had to work late or else the invitation was to attend something even Ben knew she wouldn't enjoy. It was difficult to remain silent during those moments; most of the time he wanted to throw Marco out of the room and shake Jessie until she saw reason.

On Wednesday, in the third week of his confinement, he was feeling particularly glum. Marco had ordered some tests on him the day before and was back to review the results with Ben.

"Fine...not bad...mmm...things are looking good, my friend," Marco said, flipping through the pages of data. "Of course, I'd have expected someone of your age and physical condition to show more rapid progress, but I'll take steady. You're going to fully recover, Ben. I'm convinced of that."

"You said as much the day I regained consciousness," Ben pointed out dryly. "Where's Wescott? He's the one I need to hear from."

"He's in surgery. Remember he's doing double duty to help with your caseload. He said between your patients and his, he was beginning to feel like the cataract king of the southwest."

"Dr. Collier, I could put a message in for him to come see you when he's finished in surgery," the nurse who was attending Marco offered.

Her name was Tanya something, Ben thought, trying to remember what she'd told him when she first introduced herself minutes ago. She was new. She was also shy, refreshingly so, especially considering his luck of the draw with nurses lately, and there was a natural warmth in her soft voice that reminded him of Jessie.

"No, I guess not. I suppose he'll come see me when he has something to say," Ben told her. "But thank you for offering."

"Yes, sir."

Marco cleared his throat. "Well, if you don't have any questions for me, Ben, I'd better be moving along. My schedule's packed today, as well."

"No problem. I understand." Ben felt a pang of guilt over the awkwardness that seemed to be growing between them. He was certain Marco could sense it, too, but he didn't know what to do about it. His concern for Jessie had to take precedence and if that meant his rapport with Marco had to suffer...

Marco murmured something to Tanya that Ben couldn't hear. She laughed softly, the kind of laugh a woman makes when she's being flattered by someone she's attracted to. But once the door opened and closed, Ben heard Tanya sigh.

"Is something wrong, Nurse—er, I'm sorry," Ben said sheepishly, as she began to roll his bed table back to where he could use it. "I've forgotten your name."

"Jurrow," she replied, her voice barely rising above a murmur. "Tanya Jurrow."

"Pretty."

"It was my grandmother's. Would you like me to turn on the TV before I leave, Dr. Collier? I think one of the morning news programs is still on."

Ben shook his head; but he no more than heard her turn away when he reached out, his fingertips brushing her hand. "Tanya. I don't mean to pry, but I couldn't help notice that sigh a minute ago when Dr. Tremaine left. Is something wrong?"

He could feel her hesitation and Ben almost expected her to murmur something rejecting the idea and bolt for the door. Instead, she sighed again. "No, sir, not really. I was just thinking about being new around here and how many staff members I haven't gotten to know yet . . . and how Marco—Dr. Tremaine has been especially helpful and kind to me."

"Ah."

"Oh, please don't take that the wrong way," she said quickly. "I know he's dating Jessica Holland."

"Have you met Jessie?"

"Everyone meets Jessie." Ben could hear a smile in her voice—and also a slight wistfulness. "They tell me she takes all the new girls under her wing. We had lunch together yesterday. She's a warm and generous person, isn't she?"

"You don't sound altogether thrilled to have learned that."

"Not at all! It's— I'm a bit envious, I suppose."

"Of her relationship with Dr. Tremaine?"

"You must think I'm terrible."

With a small shake of his head, Ben smiled. "What I think is that you're human. People can't help who they're attracted to, Tanya, any more than science can explain why and how the chemistry occurs in the first place."

But after she left, Ben dwelled on the phenomenon for a long time. He wasn't surprised that Marco had drawn yet another moth to his flame. Only it was too bad he wasn't taking more serious notice of Tanya's interest in him. Or was he?

No sooner did the wheels of speculation start spinning in his mind that Ben rejected the idea it spawned. What was wrong with him? Even if there was a spark between Marco and Tanya, it wouldn't be right for him to encourage them to explore it. How could he even consider it when he knew how it would hurt Jessie?

On the other hand, wouldn't it be better for her to experience a little grief now than a lot of pain later? And it wasn't as though there wouldn't be anyone around to buffer the blow. Surely she knew she could always come to *him*?

By the time Jessie came by to say good morning, Ben almost had himself convinced his theory was not only logical, but that he'd even be helping the hospital. After all, without careful handling, there was always the possibility Jessie would consider leaving. What a loss that would be to San Antonio General.

"My goodness, Doc, you can process film in this room it's so dark," Jessie said, immediately tugging up the partially opened blinds to let more sunshine in.

"These plants people keep sending you need some sun or they're going to die."

"I don't know why the nurses don't distribute them to other patients as I've asked them to do with the flowers," Ben replied absently, secretly wondering how to set his plan into motion. He would have to be careful not to be too obvious, no matter what he did.

"They have been spreading them around. The problem is that we're running out of takers, at least on this floor. How are you feeling this morning?"

Her cheery tone had him smiling. "Fine, now that you're here."

"Why thank you. But you'd better watch it, Doc. You know what a swollen head I'm liable to get from hearing such flattery."

"Go try to sell that to someone else."

"I'd rather ask what's made you so appreciative all of a sudden?"

Ben's smile wilted somewhat. "Marco dropped by."

"Why did I have to ask?"

"Don't worry, we didn't argue or anything. I'm just a bit tired of him telling me I can go ahead and start stockpiling champagne. There's nothing to celebrate yet."

Jessie seemed to consider that and said, "I heard about the latest tests he'd ordered for you. He must be optimistic."

"Someone once said that the place where optimism most flourishes is in a lunatic asylum."

"Wow. It's barely midmorning and you're almost telling jokes. Seriously, I wouldn't dismiss Marco's comments, Doc. You're definitely getting better."

Ben grimaced, though he knew he was lucky she was taking his criticism so well. What could he have been thinking? If he kept attacking Marco, all he would do is hurt her. "You want another laugh?" he asked, changing the subject. "They snuck prunes in with my breakfast and I actually ate them."

"From the looks of that tray it seems you enjoyed almost everything."

"The question is, did most of it get into my mouth or am I lying here looking like a human collage?"

Jessie carefully brushed some biscuit crumbs off his chin. "You did great. But you need another shave, Doc. Putting it off two or three days at a time only makes it harder on your skin."

"I'd rather volunteer my collapsing veins for another blood test before I let Nurse Hodges near me."

"Then let me do it."

For a moment he didn't know what to say—but only because he was wondering why he hadn't thought of the idea himself. "You have your own patients to worry about," he said, not wanting to sound too enthusiastic for fear of rousing her suspicion.

"I'm about due for my break and Tanya would cover for me if I asked her. Or are you worried that I might turn out to be worse than Nurse Hodges?"

"Of course not. I've told you before that you have good hands. You'd be a natural."

"Fine. Then it's settled. Let me get rid of this tray and tell Tanya where I'll be, then I'll come right back and we'll get to work."

It was several minutes before she returned and while he waited, Ben did a considerable amount of thinking. It gave him a twinge of guilt not to tell Jessie the reason he was intent on monopolizing her time. But after debating the issue from both sides, he rejected that guilt. Heaven knew, he had deeper concerns to deal with.

His feelings for Jessie were undergoing a serious change. He'd first noticed it on the Fourth of July. It wasn't something easy to analyze, but the truth was that ever since that day in the solarium, thinking about her had become a major preoccupation. The disturbing thing was that his thoughts weren't in any way, shape or form—pure. Maybe it went back further than the Fourth; maybe it went back to the beginning and only his moral and professional rigidness had kept him from allowing his subconscious the leeway to admit it to himself.

He was attracted to Jessie. Physically attracted. Because it had been so long since he'd experienced anything similar to this, he was bemused by the entire notion, and he found himself wanting to relish the moment, since no matter what, he had no intention of doing anything about it. How could he when nothing had changed regarding their unsuitability for each other? In fact, if anything, this realization only made things worse. Now, not only was he too old for her—not to mention all wrong for her—but he was blind, perhaps permanently so. No, he was the absolutely last person she needed in her life.

Still, how could he give her up entirely? She was his sun, she made his days bearable. He owed her for that and it was why he fully intended to do the right thing. If she was bound and determined to fall head over heels for someone, he would make sure it would be with someone who was right for her, someone who would appreciate the treasure he was getting in her.

"I'm back!"

"And not a moment too soon," Ben replied, drawing on his age and experience to hide the sudden surge of yearning he felt. "I was about to grope around for that cane my therapist gave me and hunt for you."

"Maybe I should have stayed away longer. She would have liked seeing you give it a try. Anyway, getting Tanya situated took a bit more time than I'd anticipated. Let me get a pan of water and the rest of the things we'll need and I'll be right with you."

Ben listened as she moved around in the bathroom and called, "She's very nice, isn't she?"

"Tanya? Yes, but poor thing, I don't think I've ever met anyone who's so painfully shy."

"I've noticed that myself. What does she look like?"

The room grew utterly quiet. "Why do you ask?"

"Because I can't see for myself," he reminded her dryly. "And because she seems extremely impressed with you, so I know I'm going to like her."

"Oh…well, that's very nice of you to say. How do you picture her?"

Hearing her struggle to overcome what was unmistakably a trace of jealousy, Ben grinned. "About seven-three, I suppose…orange hair…bloodshot eyes. Your normal stunning beauty."

"You!" Jessica carried the items she'd collected to the bed table and set them down. "I can't stand it when you read my mind."

"I don't read your mind, Jessie dear, I read your voice, which is about as descriptive as a seismograph diagraming a major earth tremor. But," he added gently, "if it will make you feel any better, I'm flattered that you're jealous."

"I'm not jealous," she insisted, sitting down at his side.

"All right, so what does she look like?"

"She's exactly as you described—with the exception that she weighs in at about one-ninety."

"Fascinating."

"And she's very disciplined. She always limits herself to two helpings of apple pie à la mode when they've been serving lasagna in the cafeteria."

"Stop," Ben groaned, grabbing his ribs when he couldn't repress his laughter any longer. "I apologize. Damn, Jessie, have pity. That hurts!"

"Serves you right, smarty." She silenced any further comments from him by wrapping a warm, wet towel around his face. "For your information, Tanya is lovely. She's petite and blond, and she has the prettiest fawn-brown eyes this side of an enchanted forest."

"Now this is the Jessie Holland I know. You've always been generous with your admiration for other women."

"I like her," she replied simply. "In fact I'm thinking about inviting her to move in with me. Having a two-bedroom apartment is better than living in Aunt Evelyn's mausoleum, but it's still too large for me. I get lonesome."

Ben thought about what Tanya had confided in him regarding Marco and felt the burden of having to keep the secret. "Maybe you might want to hold off extending that invitation until you know her better. What's that old adage about doing something in haste and repenting in leisure?"

"That's marrying, silly."

"Well, there are parallels."

"Your problem is that you're a hopeless skeptic," she told him, removing the towel and spraying shaving cream into her hand. With care, she smoothed it over his cheeks and chin. "I'll bet you inherited it from your ancestors, the ones who tested for witches by tying them up and dropping them into water to see if they were innocent or guilty."

"Ouch."

Jessica jerked back her hand. "Did I hurt you?"

"Considerably."

"Where?"

He tapped a finger in the vicinity of his heart. "Here." He waited—but she made no response. "What, no rebuttal?"

"I'll let you know once I figure things out."

"What's to figure?"

"You tell me. Because I'd like to know what's going on in that shrewd mind of yours. If I'd have pulled that line on you, you would have warned me against flirting with you, Doc."

Ben tried not to think about how ridiculous he must look lying there with a face coated with shaving cream. "A person can't win around you, you know that? First you complain that I'm a grouch, then when I try to turn over a new leaf, you act like I've lost my senses."

"Ah, well if it's leaves you're turning, by all means carry on."

"Imp. You know perfectly well I can't now. You've got me feeling like a man caught on Alamo Plaza in his underwear."

"Now there's a vision. You're not by chance the type who wears socks that need those funny garters, are you? Oops—careful! I almost nicked you."

"Then stop making wisecracks." Again he grabbed his ribs.

"Sorry. I keep forgetting how long it takes for those to heal."

Ben's laughter ended in a philosophical shrug. "I suppose things could have been worse. You know, the whole experience is still a blank to me."

"Well, the doctors said that it wasn't uncommon to experience selective amnesia after the kind of trauma you suffered. At least you've been spared the nightmares. You still haven't had any, have you, Doc?"

"No. But sometimes I wish I did remember something, if only to help the police try to find the guy who did this. The detective in charge of the case stops by at least once a week to check if I've remembered something more to help him."

Ben heard water splashing as Jessie gave the razor a final rinse. "I've heard about that, and that they're hoping the man is still carrying around some of your identification, so if he's picked up on another charge, maybe they can tie him to your case." She began cleaning off the remaining soap with the warm, wet towel. "They'll get him, Doc."

She spoke with such quiet confidence that he had to smile. "When you say it, I almost believe it myself," he murmured, enjoying the feel of the cloth, but more, her fingertips testing whether she'd done a good job or not. It made him think of how much better it would be to have her glide those gifted fingers over his shoulders...his chest... His throat turned dry. "I think the swelling around the stitches is going down, don't you?" he asked, trying to keep his imagination from wandering toward dangerous territory.

As if he'd invited her exploration—and maybe he had—Jessie lightly traced the healing wound on his forehead. "Dr. Foster does beautiful work. It won't be long before there's nothing left but a faint white line. You can pretend you're a dashing military officer like the ones who brandished their battle scars in those old movies."

"I'd have to grow a mustache to look authentic," he said, content to be whimsical along with her.

"Hmm..." She held her index finger over his upper lip. "I suppose you could but— Ben!" she cried, as he surprised her by lightly catching her finger between his teeth.

"Got you," he mumbled, holding her prisoner.

"You're crazy. Let go," she entreated, her voice betraying excitement as well as nervousness.

The emotions only spurred on whatever insanity it was that had taken possession of him. Suddenly he didn't want to let go. He wanted to do something wicked, outrageous—to suckle her finger, taste her as though she was the sweetest candy. He wanted to feel like a whole man again . . . with Jessie.

Instead he reached up to take her hand and brushed a tender kiss across the backs of her fingers. "Ah, Jessie . . . how ironic life is. When I had the opportunity, maybe even the right to do this, I found every excuse not to. And now, when I want—need your warmth, your generosity, you're off-limits to me."

"Y-you've been through some traumatic times. Maybe it's not really me you think you want, Doc. Maybe—"

"Can you envision me nibbling on Nurse Hodges' or Scott's finger?" he drawled.

"Ben! You're being terrible."

True. He didn't know what was coming over him. Maybe someone had made a mistake and given him another patient's medication. But even though he knew he should try to get ahold of himself, something stronger overruled his good intentions. He was tired of being the ever-so-civilized Dr. Collier. "Jessie . . . why not? For old time's sake?"

"Why not what?" she asked, her voice barely audible.

Ben gently but firmly tugged at her until she was close enough for him to frame her face with his hands. "Kiss me."

She exhaled shakily. In fact, he could begin to feel her trembling all over. He found it was unbelievably exciting.

"Why are you doing this?" Jessica whispered. "Don't you realize what you're doing to me?"

"I'm only offering you what you always wanted."

"But I—you know I'm dating Marco now."

"One kiss. He needn't know." Ben stroked her high cheekbones with his thumbs. "Think of it as a gesture of humanity." He drew her closer. "Think of it as a token of affection between two close and dear friends." He could feel her breath against his lips and drew it in hungrily. "*Dear* friends."

"No!" Jessie jerked back and out of his arms, jumped from the bed and stumbled toward the door. "I'm sorry. I can't."

"Oh, hell . . . Jessie!"

Without letting him finish, she ran out of the room and raced halfway down the hall before she realized her behavior was attracting attention. Ducking into an empty room, she adjusted her cap and her hair and ran a smoothing hand down her skirt. There was nothing, however, that she could do about her turbulent thoughts.

He'd wanted to kiss her.

Jessica glanced down at her right index finger. It still tingled from his touch, not because he'd hurt her or anything—he'd been so careful—but because she'd never indulged in loveplay like that with anyone before.

And he'd wanted to kiss her.

"I don't believe it," she moaned. "I *don't* believe I ran out of there. Am I crazy or what?"

"Taking up talking to yourself, Curly?" Marco said, tugging at a strand of her clipped back hair.

Jessica whirled around, pressing her hand to her chest. "Marco!" she cried, her expression quickly going from shocked to reproachful. "Must you always sneak up on me like that?"

Marco quirked his eyebrows. Though his dark eyes twinkled, he pretended to look indignant. "Is that any way to greet your Lambchop, your Scooterpie, your Sweet Potato?"

"Save it," Jessica replied, with a dismissive wave of her hand. "We've got problems and you might as well hear before anyone else. I'm quitting."

"Your job?"

"No, this ridiculous plan you concocted."

"*I* concocted? Wait a minute, Cupcake. If I remember correctly, if it wasn't for your—"

"Never mind," she said, remembering all too well that she wasn't without guilt herself. "What I mean is things aren't working out and you need to try a different approach to get Ben out of his depression. As of right now, I'm no longer available."

"What happened?"

"He tried to kiss me."

"Pardon?"

"Marco, this is no time to go deaf. He tried to kiss me."

"That's all?"

Jessica glared at him. "All? I'm dating you! I mean you and I are supposed to be . . . we're pretending that . . . oh, you know what I mean."

"Yeah, yeah, but I still don't get the problem. This is what you've always wanted. Why didn't you let him have his way with you, as it were?"

"There must be a fungus in the air-conditioning system that affects only men," she said, eyeing the vent above them. She took a deep breath and fixed her gaze on the grinning man before her. "*Think,* Marco. If I'd let him kiss me, how long do you think it would be before the doubts set in? Why he practically has me living on a pedestal. As far as he's concerned, I'm dependable and faithful. Would a woman like that give her heart to one man and fool around with another 'for old time's sake?'"

"On the other hand, who would have bet that old Iron Morals would poach on forbidden territory?"

"The culmination of my wildest dreams has come true. Call St. Peter and have him make me a reservation on Cloud Nine," Jessica declared, her arms spread wide. "I've finally been compared to a land mass."

"It was only an expression, Jess. What I'm trying to impress upon you is that we were both wrong about Ben. If I was you, I'd have gone with the flow, puckered up and enjoyed myself."

"Thank you, Dr. Ruth." Closing her eyes at the hopelessness of it all, Jessica groaned. "I'm sorry, Marco. I don't want to let you down, but I can't continue with this. I'm no actress. Half the time I don't even remember what's the truth and what's pretend."

"You can't quit now, you're in too deep."

"This is not the CIA, Marco. Watch me."

As she began to step around him, he caught her arm. "Wait. Can't you see? It's starting to work. He's reaching for something. You. We've succeeded in getting his mind off himself, just as we planned. Thanks to you, he's realizing what he's missing in life and he's trying to fix that."

"Think how thrilled he'll be when we tell him, 'Surprise! You didn't do any of that on your own. We tricked you into it.'"

"He'll probably thank us."

"More likely he'll make your nose look like Mount Rosa, and as for me... if I'm lucky, he'll never speak to me again. No, Marco," Jessica said, firmly shaking her head. "I can't deceive him like this."

"Jessie... please." Marco took hold of her shoulders. "You have to. Don't you understand what will happen if you walk out of his life now? What would I tell him? Believe me, he'd have questions. Either way, he'd fall right back into the pit he's been wallowing in. Maybe he'd even get worse. Don't deny you don't know that he could."

"I don't want to hear this," she cried, pressing her hands against her ears.

"You have to stay with this," Marco insisted. "His tests show a steady improvement. Whether he'll admit it or not, something's got him fighting for his health. I'll bet the bank that it's you."

"In the meantime I'm losing my mind," Jessica said bitterly, turning away from Marco's intent scrutiny. "I don't know whether to believe he's reacting this way because he really feels something for me or whether he's simply hung up on trying to get me to stop seeing *you*."

"I don't imagine it's easy," Marco said, giving her a hug in sympathy. "But do you really think you could turn your back on him? Hey, who knows, maybe you're worrying about nothing. Or maybe you can turn this to your advantage. If anyone can do it, you can." He gave her a coaxing smile. "What do you say? Are we still a team?"

She really had no choice. Even as Jessica tried to resist Marco's smile, she knew that. Yet she couldn't help thinking that Ben was going to be terribly upset, not to mention annoyed, when he discovered he'd been manipulated like a pawn. All she could do was hold on to the thought that in one respect at least, Marco was right: Ben was getting better, and she wanted to be around, *had* to be around to see him go full circle to complete recovery.

"All right," she said wearily. "But I want you to know I'm doing this against my better judgment."

"Duly noted. Now stop worrying. Nothing's going to go wrong."

As he ran off to his next assignment, Jessica stood there for several more seconds, a worried frown puckering her brow. "Why did you have to say that?" she groaned and glanced upward. Nothing like tempting Providence. "He *really* didn't mean to say it," she whispered conspiratorially.

Chapter Five

It had happened so suddenly that Ben wasn't sure he might not be imagining things. The day he'd tried to kiss Jessie, the very moment she'd twisted free and run from the room, he'd sensed a change in his vision. Not an actual clearing per se, but an awareness of light, the vaguest perception of brighter and darker shades of gray.

He kept the revelation to himself; after all, the entire experience lasted only seconds and it was another two days before it occurred again. Now five days later, there was barely time to get excited or concerned about how it would fit in with the scheme of things; Marco was standing in his room and the way he was beating around the bush, Ben was getting the feeling he was about to be evicted.

"When's the family planning to come down again to visit you?" Marco asked conversationally, while scribbling notes on Ben's file.

"They're not, at least not that I know of," Ben replied, shifting in the direction of the other man's voice. "Why?"

"Well, we've done all we can for you. The general consensus is you'd complete your recovery more comfortably in your own home. Naturally, you're under no pressure to do that, but we wanted you to be aware the option exists."

Right, Ben thought dryly. They weren't going to pressure him, but they wanted to know how soon could he vacate the premises?

He knew he shouldn't be feeling such resentment. This was what he wanted, what he thought he'd been waiting for. Yet oddly enough he couldn't accept the news without some misgivings.

"I still can't see," he reminded Marco, deciding it might be more advantageous to keep his news a secret for now.

"No. But we think that given a little more rest, and the added psychological reassurance of being in a familiar environment, that will happen soon enough. The only problem is that there's no way we can authorize your release without a reassurance that you'd have around-the-clock supervision."

Ben bristled at the notion that he needed what amounted to nothing more than a glorified baby-sitter. "Next you'll be recommending I sign up for a Seeing Eye dog."

"And waste the services of a good animal? Not hardly," Marco replied, and Ben could have sworn he was struggling not to laugh. "By the time the dog adjusted to your, er, disposition, you'd have to pass him on to someone who really needed him."

"All right," Ben replied stiffly, not about to let the younger man enjoy himself too much at his expense. "Maybe something can be arranged."

"Good. We can make the call for you. Who did you have in mind? With your sister in the late stages of pregnancy, I suppose you'll probably want us to contact your mother?"

"That won't be necessary."

"A cousin or someone we don't have on record?"

"You're certain I'm ready to be released?"

"That's right, unless you want to sign up for some elective surgery. Harrison seems to be pushing liposuction these days."

"I think you should put yourself on the waiting list for a sense of humor transplant, Tremaine," Ben said, trying to keep his temper and think of how he could work this to his benefit. "At any rate, I don't believe a relative would be as helpful as someone who was trained for emergencies."

"No, but private nurses are expensive, and they're not for everyone."

Ben was becoming increasingly convinced he was being released for reasons that were more personal than therapeutic. Perhaps all was not perfect in paradise. Could Jessie have told Marco about him trying to kiss her? "It might work for me," he countered, deciding to play out the scene. "It would, of course, depend on the nurse."

He could almost feel Marco's eyes bore into him. "You sound as though you already have someone picked out."

"Logic seems to bring one to mind."

"Jessie?"

"Jessie."

Marco had left the door open and the sound of a doctor being paged over the public address system seemed unusually loud, as was the whisper of refrigerated air being pushed through ceiling registers. Ben was as acutely aware of both, just as he was aware of Marco's hesitation. What he wouldn't give right now to see his face.

"What do you expect me to say?" Marco finally asked.

Ben contained his answering shrug to suggest mild indifference, while inside his nerves were growing more and more tense. "Whatever you like as long as you allow her to make up her own mind regarding the matter."

"You actually think I'm foolish enough to try to forbid her?"

"Forbid who what?" Jessica asked from the doorway.

They might as well have been in a cave the way the question echoed in the room. It took every ounce of control Ben had to wait and see what Marco would say—more importantly, how Jessie would react once she heard the news.

She'd been avoiding him. Oh, it was carefully done; at least it hadn't drawn anyone else's attention that he could tell. She still stopped by to say hello or to deliver a plant or a card, but only when she knew someone else was already in the room. And she always made an excuse to leave when they did.

At first, Ben had let it go; he needed time to come to terms with what he himself had done. But now he worried whether he would ever succeed in regaining the ground lost by his impulsiveness. What he couldn't do was leave here if that meant leaving Marco with a free field from which to woo Jessie.

"I'm offering Ben his freedom," Marco told her, as if he hadn't heard her question.

"That's wonderful," Jessie replied. But barely, Ben noted with pleasure, as enthusiastically as she might have sounded. "When?"

"Whenever he wants. There's a slight hitch, though. He has to make some arrangements first."

"I don't understand," she murmured.

Ben decided he was going to respond to that before Marco tried to pull something. "I'm told I need someone to stay with me to make sure I don't cut off a finger while making a sandwich or ruin this nose job by walking into a wall. It wouldn't be fair to burden my family, so I thought I would hire a professional. You never know when there might be an emergency."

"An emergency?" Jessie's voice grew vague and he could sense her turning to Marco for answers.

"We don't anticipate any," Marco reassured her.

"But it's always better to be safe than sorry," Ben added.

"Of course," Jessie murmured. "It's a good idea. Well then, congratulations are in order."

"Don't congratulate him yet," Marco drawled. "Wait until you hear who he wants as his nurse."

Once again silence fell. Ben could picture Jessie signaling her feelings to Marco. "Marco, why the droll attitude? You know she's perfect for the job."

"You forget that she'd have to take temporary leave and that's not always easy to arrange."

"We both have pull with the right people. We can help."

Marco laughed. "You think I'm crazy enough to hand her to you on a silver platter?"

"I think you're both crazy," Jessie announced. "And how dare you two talk about me as if I wasn't even in the room."

"Now, honey, relax," Marco drawled. "Don't you see what's going on? Ben's out to test us. He thinks I don't trust you to be around him. But we know better, don't we?"

"Wait a minute—are you saying you *agree* with this plan?"

"I'm not thrilled about it," he said quickly, clearly trying to correct his blunder. "But first and foremost I have to think like a doctor. I appreciate his wanting to have someone around who's not only comfortable to be with but trustworthy. Someone who'll make sure he gets the best help possible. That's you, Jess."

"Uh-huh. Could we step outside for a moment?" she asked sweetly.

Ben knew what would come of that and decided he couldn't let it happen. "Jessie, is it asking too much to steal you away from the hospital for a week or two? I'm sure that's all it would be. And Marco knows he can trust me, don't you, Marco?''

"It's *her* I'll be trusting, old boy, not you."

"Will you stop!" Jessie cried. "And I haven't said—"

"Excuse me for interrupting."

Ben recognized the voice at the doorway as belonging to Tanya. Great, he thought, if any more people came in here, they could perform one of Shakespeare's comedies.

"Dr. Tremaine, there's an urgent call for you from Dr. Prentiss," she continued.

"Thank you, Tanya. Jess—sorry," Marco told her. "This conversation will have to wait until later."

Jessica watched as Marco suavely beckoned Tanya to go on before him, giving her a warm, too warm, smile. She groaned inwardly and was secretly thankful Ben couldn't see it.

"Marco—" she called after him. But she could tell he had every intention of ignoring her. Traitor, she thought. Wretch. The man had absolutely no sense of loyalty or team support.

"Let him go, Jessie," Ben murmured behind her.

She clenched her hands into tight fists and spun around to face him. Despite her annoyance, her heart fluttered. With sunlight beaming across the room and illuminating the gold highlights in his hair, Ben looked healthier, more like his old self, and it made it all the more difficult for Jessica to resist him as she knew she must.

"Shame on you, Doc," she said, deciding not to mince words.

"You didn't tell him."

Obviously he wasn't going to beat around the bush either because Jessica immediately understood what he was referring to. "What was there to tell?" she replied, amazed she almost succeeded in achieving the casualness she'd attempted. "Nothing happened."

"Then why have you been avoiding me? And why are you afraid to come stay with me at my condominium?"

"I haven't been avoiding you, I've been busy. And I'm *not* afraid." But she had to pace the width of the room and back again to burn some of her nervous energy. "It's just that I don't think it would be right...I mean, it wouldn't look proper...oh, I can't believe you're even suggesting this!"

Ben shrugged. "You're competent. We know each other. We like each other. There wasn't a more obvious choice."

"Well, it wouldn't be fair to Marco. He might be taking this as a good sport, but deep down I know he's not happy. I could see his expression," she added, trying to forget the wicked grin the rascal had given her. She made a promise to herself to get him back for that, too.

"All right," Ben murmured. "If you're comfortable with him making all your decisions for you and choosing your friends, we'll forget it."

"He's not doing that."

"Then what's happening to us?"

"Nothing's happening to us. There *is* no us. I mean— I don't know what I mean anymore." Between Ben and Marco she was beginning to wonder if she wasn't losing her grip on reality.

"Jessie." Ben extended his hand to her. "Come here."

"No way."

"Why not? The door's still open, isn't it? So I'm not about to try anything. I wouldn't anyway. Not when you're obviously upset with me. All I want to do is explain myself to you. Please," he murmured huskily, his smile coaxing. "Come sit with me for a moment."

"I should have my head examined," she replied, edging closer and finally sitting down on the very edge of the bed. But she ignored the hand that beckoned for hers. "Start talking."

Ben's expression turned amused. "How delightfully petulant you can be at times."

"Listen, buster, you're walking a fine line here. I'm no more petulant than you are harmless." She glanced down at her watch. "You've got exactly sixty seconds to say your piece and then I'm out of here."

"Coward."

"Sticks and stones, Doc."

"Jessie, can't we get past that unfortunate episode? I've tried to apologize. I've admitted that I let things get out of hand. What else do I have to say to win back your friendship?"

"Tell me why—the real reason why—you want me to stay with you at your place?"

"I already did."

"That does it," she muttered, beginning to rise.

Ben reached out to stop her. "All right! I confess. I want to make sure that you have some time away from Marco before things get too serious between you two. That's all. I just want to buy you time."

Jessica considered that while searching his face. He looked sincere. Even apologetic. She would have been happier if he'd looked as heartsick as she felt. Didn't he have any idea what being around him twenty-four hours a day would do to her?

Her gaze fell to his mouth. "If I considered doing this for you, would you give me your word you wouldn't try anything?" She knew giving in would prove she was crazy, but maybe if she had his promise...otherwise, she didn't think she could resist him if he tempted her again.

"Yes." He sighed. "Blame it on cabin fever, Jessie—and a bit on your being such a dear friend to me—but I realize now that it would still be wrong for me to encourage anything between us. I may not think Marco's right for you, but I know I'm not either."

Back to square one, Jessica thought, wincing at the stab of pain that attacked her heart. This would be a perfect time to come clean, to tell him everything she and Marco had done to try to help him. But she couldn't bring herself to do it.

Regardless of what her intentions had been, she knew he would be furious to know she'd deceived him, and she couldn't bear thinking of someone else accompanying him to his home, taking care of him.

"You're extremely quiet. Is a decision that difficult?"

"You have no idea."

"I suppose I could give you a few hours."

"That won't be necessary. I've made up my mind," she said, trying to ignore that he'd found one of her hands and was stroking his thumb across the back in what he obviously thought was a soothing gesture. It only served to make her ache for more. "I'll do it."

He broke into a relieved, almost boyish smile. "You won't be sorry, Jessie. I'll be a model patient."

"Maybe I should rent a video camera and record that for posterity. I could make a fortune selling copies of the tape to the nurses around here who've come to think otherwise."

"In that case I'll do my best to be extra good."

Jessica, she thought grimly, now would be a good time to start worrying.

It took two days for Jessica to arrange for leave, but on Thursday morning she finally pushed Ben's wheelchair out of San Antonio General and to her already-packed car. As the hospital's automatic doors rolled closed behind them, she took a deep breath of the steamy air and exhaled, trying to purge some of her nervousness. They had received more than a few curious looks and from some of the staff who knew what was going on amused ones. Let Marco handle the explanations, she thought mutinously. It was the least he could do since he helped get her into this.

"You're going to give me a complex if you sigh like that again," Ben said, as she paused to open the passenger side of her small car.

"Don't mind me. I was only running through a list in my mind trying to decide if I'd remembered everything. Okay, now easy does it, shift your feet to the ground and grab hold of the car door before you stand."

"I'm blind not incapacitated," he replied, rising with surprising agility.

Still, Jessica held her breath as he eased himself into the cramped car. Despite his caution, his neatly combed hair got mussed when he came too close to the outer steel frame. It could have been worse, she thought, exhaling in relief. "Let me return the chair and I'll be right back," she told him.

Halfway up the sidewalk, she was met by a candy striper who took the wheelchair from her. Thanking her, Jessica returned to the car.

It felt both exhilarating and strange to have Ben so close. As she reached for her seat belt she stole a quick glance at him. Except for a slight pallor, he looked the picture of health in his white polo shirt and tan pants. They'd been among the things his mother had brought for him. Jessica had considered changing out of her uniform, but decided against it after wondering if it might not invite raised eyebrows from Marco. At least she'd thought to wear a pants suit today.

Something about the way Ben was blinking behind the sunglasses she'd picked up for him caught her attention. "There's a strong glare this morning. Are you able to sense it?"

"No." He turned his head away from her. "It's only a bit of dust or something."

Disappointed, Jessica started the engine and hoped he wasn't going to slip into one of his quiet moods.

She'd memorized his home address way back when she'd first gotten a crush on him; as a result, she was able to drive there without asking for directions. If Ben was surprised, he made no comment. Along the way she made a point to tell him about interesting things she noticed. But he didn't seem overly enthused about that either.

"Hey," she finally complained at a red traffic light. "I'm the one who's supposed to have a case of nerves here. Why are you so quiet?"

"It struck me that I'm taking you to my home, and that there's a man out there who not only has a set of keys to my car, and my condominium, he has my wallet with my address. What if he decided to pay another visit? I wouldn't be able to protect you."

"Oh, Ben." Forgetting everything she'd promised herself about maintaining her distance, Jessica reached over and squeezed his hand. "I should have told you sooner. Your father had all your locks changed while they were down here visiting you. Besides that, the police have been notified you're going home today and they're going to increase their patrols. We'll be perfectly safe."

"Thank heaven. I can't tell you what a relief it is to hear that."

As he turned toward her, she found herself looking at her reflection in his lenses. She'd removed her nurse's cap and barrette before leaving the hospital and her hair tumbled around her shoulders. They

could be two people out on a date ... or even returning from their honeymoon, she fantasized.

Someone honked behind them.

Jessica gave herself a mental shake and returned her
attention to the road.

Ben's condominium was in a new development only
ten minutes from the hospital. The pink stucco walls
and gray tile roofs of the buildings echoed the Spanish flavor maintained throughout the city and the
grounds were lavishly landscaped with tropical shrub-
bery and trees.

Jessica had seen it before, after her operation when
she'd passed by with a driving school instructor. She'd
loved the place on sight and for months afterward had
daydreamed about being invited inside. What would
Ben say if he knew a longtime dream of hers was about
to come true?

After depressing the remote control button that
signaled his garage door to open, Jessica eased her
Chevy in beside the BMW his father had collected
from the police station pound weeks ago after he'd
located Ben's second set of keys. "Well, here we are,"
she said, shutting off the engine and releasing her seat
belt. "I'll go unlock the door. Then we'll get you and
all this paraphernalia inside."

"I'll help."

"That's okay. There's hardly anything in your suitcase and I packed light since I know I can always hop
over to my place if I need something. All you have to
concentrate on is making sure you get plenty of rest.
I'll worry about getting us settled."

"Jessie, I've been resting for weeks," Ben told her dryly. "I need to move, and I didn't ask you to come here so I could have a live-in maid."

She didn't want to argue. They'd worked too hard to get to this point, such as it was. With a murmur of agreement, she let him carry his own suitcase, while she took hers, and taking his hand led him inside.

They entered a short hallway with the utility room off to one side and a half bath on the other. Next came the kitchen, a spacious, modern room with Wedgewood blue cabinets and an adjoining dinette area complete with a skylight.

"This is wonderful. And look at all these appliances."

"I have this thing for gadgets."

"You like to cook?"

"Sometimes. How do you feel about Oriental cuisine?"

"The mere mention of it makes me drool."

Ben chuckled as he followed the counter line with his hand to feel his way to the living room. "If you're game, I can talk you through a great recipe for chicken with walnuts."

"Make it Texas pecans and you're on."

They continued through the living room, which was darker than the kitchen with its use of richly stained furnishings and elegant yet restful shades of blue and green. The collection of watches and small clocks in the side cabinets of a grandfather clock made Jessica chuckle.

"I should have known a time-conscious Virgo like you would collect timekeepers."

"In that case you've probably already figured out that one of my bedrooms has been converted into a study," he teased, slowly feeling his way to the next room down the hall. With the wall-to-wall bookshelves he'd had built in, it was now a cozy cubbyhole. A rolltop desk, a few antique, wooden file cabinets and a well-used recliner were all the furnishings the room could hold.

"I imagined you'd have an office away from your office. But there aren't as many magazines and journals as I thought you would have," she said, noting a small selection of back issues on one shelf.

"I've had to cut down because of space and reading time limitations," he replied with a sheepish smile.

The last two rooms were bedrooms. Ben indicated the one on the right as the guest room. The walls were painted a shell white, the curtains and the queen-sized bedspread were done in a green and yellow swirling watercolor design. Though simple, Jessica knew she would feel welcome here, an intuition that was reinforced when she spotted the sunken tub in the adjoining bathroom.

"It's lovely. I'll be more than comfortable here," she murmured, glancing back at him as he stood almost hesitantly in the hallway. His relieved smile pushed all her doubts about taking this assignment from her mind. "Let's put your case in your room."

The master bedroom was the darkest room in the house. Ben explained it was planned that way for when his schedule demanded he try to catch up on his sleep during daylight hours. The navy, burgundy and gold furnishings were of an austere but impressive Eastern design. Books and a good reading lamp took over most of the shelving in the headboard of the massive bed, and a huge, illuminated terrarium in the navy-and-gold bathroom gave the room the illusion of having a window.

"It's a wonderful place," Jessica murmured appreciatively. "Did you have help with the decorating?"

"My mother." Ben's expression turned wry. "She's a frustrated decorator at heart and when I bought the place, I flew her down for a week to give me a hand. We argued about almost everything, but she finally caught on to what I wanted. In the end I had to phone my father and beg him to order her to come home, but it was fun." Ben followed her back down the hall. "Do you really like it? You don't think it's too—stodgy?"

"It's beautiful and elegant, and if you remind me one more time that I've used that kind of word to describe you, my face is going to stay permanently red from embarrassment."

"Are you blushing? Let me see." Before Jessica could react, Ben reached over and touched the back of his hand to her cheek. His subsequent whistle was soundless. "You're right. I think you passed fire engine red and went straight to berry berry."

Jessica intended to laugh, but the sound became a painful knot locked in her throat; she would never have guessed that joy could hurt so much. He was doing it—he was trying to *play*. Did he have any idea what it meant to her to see this effort after all his insistence that he was too old, too set in his ways to change and be lighthearted? It was a moment she wanted to cherish, but she knew she needed to move.

Only her legs didn't seem to be paying attention to her brain's instructions, despite the heartache she knew she was inviting. The dreamer in her insisted on greedily drawing on the moment.

Then the front doorbell sounded, jerking Jessica back to reality. Exhaling shakily, she excused herself and, sidestepping Ben, went to answer it. She told herself that the echoing sigh behind her was nothing more than wishful thinking.

Chapter Six

"Morning, ma'am. Sir." The uniformed policeman at the door gave a courteous tip of his hat. "I'm sorry for the intrusion."

As Ben placed a concerned hand on her shoulder, Jessica covered it with her own to reassure him. "That's all right, Officer...?"

"Grimes." His gauging glance shot to Ben and back to her. The smile he offered was apologetic, which made his face even more boyish, but he was brisk and businesslike when he drew out his identification for her inspection. "I'm one of the officers patrolling this neighborhood. We just received a report that the man suspected of attacking Dr. Collier has been spotted only a few miles from here. Since we'd heard the doctor was returning home today, we thought we'd inform you before you heard it on TV or the radio, and to let you know we're beefing up our patrols."

"That's very thoughtful of you."

"I don't mean to raise unnecessary concern, ma'am, but if possible, it would be best to stay inside as much as possible until we have this situation resolved. If you see or hear anything suspicious, call 911 immediately."

"We will, Officer Grimes, and thank you very much." Jessica closed the door and secured the deadbolt. "Well, that cancels the idea I had to go to the grocery store while you take a nap." She tried to keep her voice casual because she could already feel the tension emanating from Ben.

Unsurprisingly, he swore under his breath. "I should have had my head examined for bringing you here."

"I believe we've already had this discussion." After testing if the lock was secure, Jessica took hold of Ben's arm and directed him toward the living room. "Everything's going to be fine. You heard what the policeman said. Besides, I don't believe they really think that man will come here."

"Just the same, I want you to promise me you'll stay close, all right?"

"I knew it," she teased, deciding it would be best if she tried to change the subject. "We haven't been here a half hour yet and you're already propositioning me. I should have known you couldn't keep your word."

Ben looked momentarily startled, then he broke into a rueful smile. "Behave. You know what I mean. Sleeping for instance—I want you to leave your bedroom door open so I can hear you. Under the circumstances closing a door around me is an empty gesture anyway."

"Maybe. Maybe not. Depends on if you snore."

"Tell you what," Ben countered, just as smoothly, "how about if we compare notes in the morning?"

You asked for that. Jessica groaned inwardly and thought of the sleep she was certainly not going to get. It was hard enough knowing he would be only yards away from her, but to be able to actually hear him breathing, while all the while wanting to feel the rise and fall of his chest as she slept in his arms . . .

She took a steadying breath. "At this point I think our primary concern should be what is or isn't in the refrigerator."

"Knowing my mother, we're in trouble. She undoubtedly emptied the thing in order to keep busy while she was here. In fact if it contains more than a box of baking soda and a couple of bottles of mineral water, I'll be amazed. The freezer might not be a total loss, though."

They'd gotten as far as the living room and Jessica paused by one of the couches. Shifting her hands to his shoulders, she pushed lightly. "Sit. I'll find out. At any rate, there's always the yellow pages. I can order takeout. In the meantime you should rest."

"I told you before I'm not tired."

"Who do you think you're kidding? You look as though you've been whacked in the face with a powder puff full of cake flour."

"Jessie, I've been lying in bed for weeks. My backside is beginning to feel like one solid sore."

"Why didn't you say something? Come with me. I have some medicated cream that—"

Despite her tug on his arm, Ben stayed rooted in place. "No way. You can give it to me when I go to bed and I'll put it on myself."

"For goodness' sakes. This is no time to get modest. I'm here as your nurse, remember?"

"I wouldn't care if you were here as my doctor."

Jessica tried to be annoyed, but she knew what was behind his resisting her, and that brought a slow twinkle to her eyes. "Fine. Stay in pain and follow me around like a wounded puppy, if you want. I'll still be here when you drop."

"You'll have a long wait."

The trace of bravado in his voice made her chuckle. "The more opportunity to watch you sweat, my dear," she called over her shoulder, as she headed for the kitchen.

It turned out that not only was the refrigerator almost empty, the freezer wasn't in much better shape. In the end, Jessica took out two steaks to defrost for dinner and called a delicatessen that delivered. Besides ordering soup and sandwiches for lunch, she purchased an assortment of supplies to tide them over until she could get to a store herself.

One thing she quickly realized was that she needn't have worried about time dragging or things being slightly awkward between her and Ben. Jessica discovered that at least for the next few days getting familiarized with the place would make time race by. As for her rapport with Ben, as long as she maintained the cheeky banter he was accustomed to from her, they seemed to be able to avoid getting into sticky territory.

But by that night, Jessica was too tired to be concerned with anything except getting off her aching feet. As the grandfather clock chimed nine, she slipped off her shoes and curled up cross-legged on the couch. Odd, she mused, how she'd been caring for only one man, yet her enthusiasm to please him had her as exhausted as if she'd had one of her busiest days at the hospital.

Across from her on the other couch, Ben lay strategically on his side, halfhearted in his attempt to champion one of the wire puzzles someone at the hospital had given him to help pass time. A CD was playing in the background. Jessica could have done with something less somber than the cello solo. From the looks of things, Ben could, too. It seemed while she'd been washing their dinner dishes in the kitchen, Ben had allowed his mood to drop lower than the bass notes now being played.

Sipping on a last cup of coffee, she watched him succeed in separating the puzzle. "You're getting pretty good at that."

"It's not surprising, since I've had plenty of opportunity to practice."

She grimaced at the cynicism with which he spoke. "How do you generally spend your evenings, when you're not working late at the hospital?"

"You mean how did I used to," he corrected.

"You will again."

She could tell by the set of his jaw that he was tempted to contradict her, but apparently he reconsidered. "I try to catch up on my reading." The smile that followed was more of a smirk. "My life-style isn't exactly as adventurous as Marco's, Jessie."

There he went again thinking she compared them. She wished she could tell him that the only things she and Marco had in common were an affection for the ice-cream sandwiches in the hospital cafeteria—and *him*. But wouldn't that set things buzzing. "I like to read myself, especially after a hard day," she told him instead.

"I meant mostly medical journals."

"Well, I have my share of those, plus nursing magazines and newsletters and such. But don't you break the monotony with a juicy mystery novel occasionally?"

His expression turned indulgent. "Thrillers. The modern man's Jules Verne."

"Mercy, I hope not. Some of the plotlines in those things are enough to give me nightmares."

"Which succeeds in getting your mind off the nightmares at work." Tossing the puzzle onto the coffee table, Ben sat up and reached for his own coffee. "What do you prefer to read?"

"You'll probably laugh. When I want to forget everything, I fill my tub with hot water, pour in an outrageous amount of bubble bath, then snatch up a romance novel and soak until I'm—oh, medium rare."

He closed his eyes. "I had to ask."

"No jokes, Doc. I wasn't hard on you."

"I'm not criticizing," he said gently. When he reopened his eyes, Jessie was momentarily convinced he was looking straight at her. "I was bemoaning the sudden vividness of my imagination."

"Oh."

"The understatement of the century." His coffee sloshed over onto his saucer and, seeming at a loss as to what to do, he set the cup and saucer back on the table. But that left him with the predicament of having empty, idle hands. "Do you buy your bubble bath scented like hyacinths, too?"

"Yes." Her voice was little more than a whisper, the sound barely discernible to her own ears over that of her thumping heart.

"I don't have any...bubble bath, I mean."

"No," she replied quickly. "I didn't imagine you did. It's not something a man thinks to put on his shopping list."

"Not really. Though it would probably be just the thing one could use to relax sore muscles after putting in a long day. As you have for example."

"I don't feel too badly," she murmured, deciding that saying something, anything, was better than allowing silence to settle in. She was afraid her imagination would only get her into trouble if there was too much silence.

It stretched between them anyway.

"How do you feel about lemons?" he asked after what seemed a lifetime and a half.

Jessica had just sipped at her coffee and inadvertently sent some down her windpipe. Choking and coughing, it took her several seconds to reply. "Fine.

Umm . . . I like them on fish," she wheezed, not sure she was following him and trying desperately to ignore what her fertile mind was conjuring. "And I liked the way my mother used to grate a little peel into her cake frosting."

Ben clasped and reclasped his hands. "My housekeeper buys some lemony smelling dish-washing liquid."

"Good for her."

"You don't understand. The reason I mentioned it is because someone told me they use it as bubble bath for their kids."

"Clever." Was the room getting warmer or was it nerves? "The rinse cycle should be interesting, though I don't suppose they have to worry about water spots." When he failed to reply, Jessica uttered an entreating sound. "That was supposed to be a joke."

Ben only shook his head. "I didn't mean to make you nervous."

"Who's nervous?" she asked with an awkward laugh.

"You are, and I don't blame you, especially after what I'd promised. It was insane to say, to think . . . forget it."

"I'm not nervous," Jessica said again, but this time her voice held more confidence. She watched Ben draw in a deep breath.

"This blindness is worst to cope with at night when I'm trying to sleep. You see, there's no change. No sense of relief. I thought . . . if I could hear you enjoying your bath . . ." This time he laughed self-consciously. "This must sound absurd to you."

"It sounds very honest," she insisted gently. "Tell me. Please."

"I think you could get my mind off myself, Jessie. I think you could get me past the fear."

Tears filled Jessica's eyes. She ached to rush over to him, sit at his feet and press her cheek to his white-knuckled hands. Never had she heard anything so heartwrenching or endearing.

She forced down the lump in her throat and rose. "As I said, a bubble bath sounds exactly like what I need."

He was still sitting there when she returned from the kitchen clutching the economy-size plastic bottle to her chest. "I'll get the lights later. Why don't you turn in? You look tired."

"All right."

"Goodnight, Doc. Sweet dreams."

"Yes," he murmured absently. "Sweet dreams."

He must have been crazy to think it would help. Help drive him out of his mind, that was about all it was doing.

It was hours since she had slipped into her own bed, but as Ben lay in his, isolated in his darkness, he could still hear in his mind Jessie's bathwater running, even as he now listened to her sleeping. He recalled for the tenth time how she'd sighed with delight when she'd stretched out in the tub...the musical trickle of droplets...the whisper of cloth over her skin...the reverberating silence when she stood to dry herself. Oh, his imagination was keen. And he was a fool.

Instead of giving him peace from the prison he was shrouded in, he'd condemned himself to an added sentence of physical agony. Reminded of things he'd been denying himself, his mind's eye conjured images of a bubbly paradise. He imagined Jessie, her lithe body, sleek and shimmering, her dark curls piled high on her head with tendrils escaping to caress her neck and shoulders, as he longed to do. What he wouldn't give to really see her like that. In the car this morning his vision had tried to clear. For a few, all too brief seconds he'd had a foggy sort of glimpse of her. As grateful as he was, he sucked in a deep breath and bit off a groan. While it had been more than he'd dared hope for, it was hardly enough.

Restless, he turned toward his digital clock, then swore because he forgot he couldn't see the numbers. Damn, but it was hot. Despite wearing only the bottoms of a pair of pajamas, his body was feverish and damp. When was the last time the air conditioner had kicked on? His throat was as dry as if he'd been trekking through the hill country.

Reaching toward where he usually kept a cup of water, he found the spot empty. Once again disgusted with himself, he rolled onto his back. Preoccupied with thoughts of Jessie he'd even forgotten to complete that simple routine.

Certain he'd lose his mind if he stayed in bed another minute, Ben threw back the bed sheet and pushed himself to his feet. The kitchen, he told himself, was on the opposite side of the house. There he wouldn't be able to hear her. He would find something biting cold to drink. And then he might find peace by spending the rest of the night on the couch.

Pausing to listen at her doorway was a gift he awarded himself for his honorable intentions. She wasn't sleeping restfully either. He rationalized it was because she was in a strange bed, a dangerous man was prowling the streets of the city and her normal routine had been disrupted, thanks to his interference. His concern for her. His selfishness.

Could he dare hope she was dreaming of him?

Maybe she was dreaming of Marco.

No doubt about it, he thought feeling his way down the hall, he was losing it.

He skirted an armchair and the floor lamp beside it. At the stereo he would make a sharp left turn. Until now he'd never noticed what a clean ninety-degree angle he'd arranged in the furniture's floor plan. There it was . . . now he had only to turn left and in about three steps . . .

"What the—!"

His foot came in contact with something hard and cold, his chest with something feathery. But in trying to jerk away from it, his toe got caught and he lost his balance. It all happened quickly, leaving him with no time to cry out; one second he was thrusting the thing away from him, the next he was crashing to the floor.

"Ben?"

Through his dazed senses he heard Jessie call him. Then she was beside him on the carpet—he thanked heaven for the carpet—almost impaling him as she tried to remove what he realized was a brass planter that shouldn't have been standing like a sentry in the middle of the living room but against the wall.

"Are you all right? You nearly gave me heart failure."

"Imagine how I feel," he replied drolly.

"Are you hurt?"

"I will be if— Jessie, will you stop yanking on that. The foot on this stand is about to remove one of my kidneys."

"Sorry. I'm only trying to get it out of your way."

"How did it get here in the first place?"

"I guess I moved it. After my bath I came out here to shut off the lights and . . . it simply didn't look right where it was. I'd planned to warn you in the morning."

"I'll consider myself warned."

"Well, how was I to know you were going to get up in the middle of the night? By the way, why are you?"

Ben decided he would almost rather face his mugger than answer that question. "It's hot," he muttered, pulling what he identified as a part of a palm frond out of his mouth. "I wanted a drink."

"Then let me help you get to your feet and into the kitchen. Here, lean on me," she insisted, when he tried to do it on his own. "Stay to your right so you don't step into the dirt that spilled out of the pot. Blast, I'm sorry about the mess."

"Just promise me you won't get any ideas about dragging out a vacuum cleaner," Ben told her, wondering if he looked half as foolish as he felt. "It can wait until morning."

"I don't blame you for being angry with me."

"I'm not angry. I only wanted to get something to drink and then climb back into bed. You should do that yourself." Please he prayed, feeling himself nearly leaning into the scent of lemons that lured him. "I'll be all right."

"It'll go faster if I help."

The only thing bound to go fast were his nerves, Ben thought as struggling to get to his feet, his hand brushed against her bare thigh. Don't do it, he ordered himself. Don't dare wonder what she's wearing.

"I hadn't realized what a bright moon there is tonight," Jessie said, leading him into the kitchen. "We won't need to turn on any lights."

"Fine. It would probably attract the police anyway."

"Oh, right. I don't think I'd like to have to explain this to them. So what can I get you?"

Ben wasn't much of a drinker, but feeling her brush against him to get to the cupboard where the glasses were kept, he began to think a double of something potent sounded appealing. "Did you notice if there was any juice? If there isn't, ice water will do."

"I made some juice from frozen orange concentrate. Give me just a second."

The air shifted again as she zipped from the island counter to the refrigerator and back again. Like a hummingbird, he thought, a warm feeling of tenderness mingling with his sexual frustration.

"Here you go." Taking his hand, she closed it around a tall tumbler. The outside was already sweating from the frigid contents.

Ben took a long greedy drink and, sighing, rolled the glass across his forehead. "That hit the spot."

"You did feel warm when I helped you up," Jessie murmured with concern. "Let me double-check."

Before he could stop her, she placed her hand to his forehead. "Jessie, it isn't necessary."

"Dear heaven, what's happened to you? You're on fire."

Immediately turning into the professional, she checked his pulse and rattled off the usual questions. Did he feel nauseous? Was he dizzy? He almost groaned because each question was followed by a concerned touch to his cheek, to his chest... Jessie was a toucher, a trait he normally found endearing, but right now it was sheer agony.

"Maybe my ribs are a bit more tender than before," he admitted, in order to end her third degree. It was, he realized with a sinking heart, an invitation to havoc.

"It's these darned bandages," she muttered, inspecting them. "They must be slipping and pressing on a spot that's still sensitive."

No, Ben replied silently, *she* was. In fact she was barely touching him and already his skin felt as though it was blistered. She moved an inch lower and his throat locked on a groan.

"Right there?" she murmured sympathetically. "Maybe you caught one of the legs on the brass planter when you fell."

"I've already forgotten about that."

"Doc, I can't tell you how badly I feel about this."

"You can't possibly feel worse than I do."

"If I hadn't moved that silly thing…let's go to your room and I'll redo the bandage. Maybe it'll help."

"Trust me, it won't."

"You can be so stubborn."

"And you can be so dense." He lifted his hands to her hair. "Jessie, listen to me. What I'm trying to impress upon you is that I don't want to go *anywhere* with you."

"Why?" she asked, her voice relaying her bewilderment and hurt.

"Because I don't much feel like being the responsible and respectable Dr. Collier tonight and if you keep pushing me, I may end up proving that to you. Understand?"

"I—oh. Yeah, it's sinking in."

"At last. So now why don't you do us both a favor and go to bed as I've asked."

Instead Jessie tilted her head so that her cheek nestled into his left palm. "Are you sure? What if I forget to tell you about something else I might have moved? For all you know there could be a veritable mine field out there in the living room waiting for you. Maybe I should stay close."

Ben's answering smile was strained. "Has anyone ever told you that you're dangerous?"

"Doc." An uncharacteristic cynicism underscored Jessie's abrupt laugh. "I've been called cute and fun and even pretty. But no man's ever called me dangerous."

"Then why, when I touched you here," he murmured, dropping one hand to skim the same smooth thigh he'd touched before, "did I feel as if I was being overwhelmed by something I don't think I'm ever going to recover from?'' When she caught his hand, his smile mirrored his deeper experience. ''What *do* you wear to bed, Jessie?'' he whispered, effortlessly easing from her grasp and inching his fingers upward, finally finding a straight simple hem near her hip.

With a sound of distress Jessie rested her forehead on his shoulder. ''Sorry to disappoint you, Doc, but there's nothing remotely sexy about this University of Texas T-shirt.''

''Think so? Don't underestimate the appeal of cotton. On certain raven-haired sprites it can be unbearably appealing.''

She raised her head and Ben could sense she was searching his face. ''Maybe you should pinch me so I'll awaken and stop dreaming.''

''Maybe you should hush and kiss me instead.'' He lowered his head and brushed his lips against hers once, then again before murmuring, ''Still think you're asleep?''

''No... because in my dreams I *am* dangerous and you don't kiss me as if I were made of rice paper and angel hair.''

Knowing he was fast approaching the edge of his restraint, Ben filled his hands with her hair and drew her head back a little farther. ''Damn it, Jessie, you have a mouth on you that would tempt a saint.''

''You'll do,'' she murmured, pressing her lips to his.

Ben felt as though a tidal wave had hit him straight on. But he relished the sensation, reached for more by answering Jessie's impassioned kiss with an equal and deep-seated honesty of his own. Desire burst free like a geyser, bathing him in sensations he never knew himself capable of feeling. He wanted to savor the moment, bring her every ounce of pleasure he could conceivably give her; but even as he acknowledged this, his own long-suppressed needs had him burying his face at her throat and stifling a groan.

"Jessie…sweet, sweet Jessie. You have no idea how many times I wanted to do this."

"Tell me."

The eagerness and honestly in her voice, as well as the delightful tremor he felt when he nuzzled a sensitive spot near her ear, had him laughing huskily. "I'd rather show you."

He claimed her lips again, thrilling to the awareness that her mouth fit so perfectly to his. His heart filled to overflowing when, without hesitation, she opened to his deeper exploration. His sweet Jessie, his own angel. Framing her face with his hands, he sought to show her how deeply and intensely he felt about her.

When she moaned softly and slipped her hands around his neck, he murmured his encouragement. "Closer. Come closer. I want your body completely against mine." Aware she was still being cautious of hurting him, he tightened his own arms until his bruised ribs protested with sharp needlelike pricks. But even that was welcome because it meant he was alive.

"Doc." Jessie sighed, as he nibbled and licked at her lips.

"Say my name," he demanded with a more ardent caress. "I want to know this isn't pity or misplaced feelings. Say it quickly. Now."

"Ben, you know it's not."

Before she could say any more he crushed his mouth to hers. He didn't need or want to hear anything else, and he definitely didn't want to think about the ramifications of this moment. Later he would whip himself raw with his conscience. Right now he needed to hold this slender, precious woman, seek and offer a corner of heaven. Nothing had changed; he was still the wrong man for her. But the feelings in his heart were right and he would use them to show her how it could be, should be between a man and woman.

"Ah, Jessie...do you see what I mean now? How can you believe you feel anything for Marco when you respond to me like this?"

She froze as if he'd thrown ice water on her. "What did you just say?" she whispered aghast.

Too late, Ben realized how badly he'd phrased his words. "I didn't mean that the way it sounded."

"Never mind how it sounded." She wrenched herself out of his arms. "Did you kiss me to make a *point?*"

"No, of course not. But you can't deny the point is a legitimate one."

"That's unbelievable." She spoke so softly, yet her voice shook. Whether from fury or tears, Ben couldn't tell, but he cursed his blindness anew. "To think I thought you were so good, so kind, so much better than other men."

"I've never pretended or aspired to be a demigod," he protested, uncomfortably aware that he'd enjoyed and, yes, encouraged her admiration. Anyway, why worry about a fall from a pedestal when even the floor beneath his feet didn't feel all that stable.

"But you did present yourself as a man of principle. What a naive idiot I am to have believed you. How far would you have gone to prove you could take my mind off Marco?"

"Jessie, I wasn't thinking about anything but you. If you'd give me a moment to explain—"

"Save it," she muttered, spinning away and stomping out of the kitchen.

Ben tried to follow, but immediately rammed his shoulder into the doorjamb. Bending from the waist in pain, he swore eloquently. "Jessie, for the love of heaven, will you wait a minute? You're going to have me back in the hospital if you keep this up."

"Fine! I hope they put you in a body cast. And you can be sure this time I won't get within five miles of your room!"

He stiffened, anticipating the sound of her bedroom door slamming. She'd once mentioned something about Taureans having nasty tempers and that she was particularly concerned with containing hers. Instead he heard a firm but controlled thud, followed by the click of the lock.

It was the click that got to him. Ben pressed his forehead against the woodwork. He deserved and would have welcomed a window-shuddering slam. Being locked out sounded far more final and that filled him with dread.

Chapter Seven

The stinker.

It was past one in the morning before Jessica calmed herself enough to take a rational look at what had happened, let alone come to *that* summation. At first all she wanted to do was pack her suitcase and leave. Hurt and angry, she'd felt it impossible to consider spending another minute under the same roof with the wretch.

But leaving, of course, was unthinkable. Even if there hadn't been a potential threat of danger to him, how could she desert Ben in his condition? Textbooks were filled with case studies of sightless people who'd learned to manage on their own, but that kind of self-sufficiency took time. This was his first night out of the hospital. He wasn't anywhere near ready to face that prospect, not physically nor psychologically.

But, oh, the man knew how to make her furious. He'd been so clever getting under her defenses with that I-can't-sleep routine, only to point out—after he'd all but reduced her to putty in his hands—that her behavior wasn't proper for a woman supposedly mad about another man. For a split second he'd almost had her believing she should have felt guilty. He'd had her so caught up in him, in his magic, she'd almost believed she had indeed been unfaithful to Marco. Once she'd gotten her wits about her, however, she'd wanted to take a swing at that perfectly squared chin of his. How dare he be able to come out of that kiss thinking so clearheadedly!

What finally got her past her anger was her conscience. Somewhere between hoping he wouldn't sleep a wink and entertaining the idea of taking a vow of eternal celibacy, she reminded herself that the only reason Ben had asked her here was because she had engaged in some duplicity of her own.

If she hadn't pretended to have feelings for Marco, Ben would never have felt compelled to save her from herself. That didn't solve the problem concerning his stubbornness about their suitability to each other, nor his rejection of her feelings for him, but it put it all in a clearer perspective.

Only a clear perspective didn't do much for her—at least it didn't make her feel half as good as she did when she was in Ben's arms. And understanding his good intentions wasn't going to make him realize how wrong he was either. If she was going to make him accept that they were right for each other—and if tonight's episode was anything to go by, she was more certain than ever they were—then she was going to have to throw caution to the wind and take some major risks.

The primary one was that she wasn't going to hide her feelings for Ben any longer. How she intended to pull that off, she had no idea since a confession about her and Marco would undoubtedly only earn her an invitation to leave. But what if she made it impossible for him to ignore her or, more precisely, ignore the fact that he had feelings for her?

Come hell or high water, Dr. Benedict Collier was going to have to face the truth. She loved him. It wasn't puppy love or infatuation; it was stomach-twisting, heart-shaking love, and *nothing* he could do was going to change that.

Her new resolve brought a blissful smile to her lips. She was still smiling when she snuggled around her pillow and slipped into a contented sleep.

Coffee. He needed coffee.

Having no idea what time it was, but convinced he couldn't lie in that torture chamber of a bed a moment longer, Ben cautiously felt his way to the kitchen and groped around for the coffee machine. His head was pounding as if he'd actually consumed the bourbon he'd rejected last night. His nerves were stretched so tight they should have been humming. As he found the glass pot and groped his way to the sink, he decided he didn't feel much better than when he'd regained consciousness after the attack. He hoped Jessie appreciated what she'd done to him; a man in his condition didn't need this added stress.

When he filled the pot to what he judged with his finger was the correct level, he replaced it on the machine and went to the pantry to hunt down a box of premeasured packets. Thanking the scientific mind that had come up with that bit of modern technology, he reached into the first shelf where he normally kept the coffee.

It wasn't there.

Ben searched again. Tea . . . sugar and flour canisters . . . what was the vegetable oil doing on this shelf? "Damnation, the coffee's supposed to be *here,* " he muttered in frustration.

"It's on the counter next to the machine."

He swung around, embarrassment competing with his relief that she'd deigned to even speak to him. "Well, what's it doing there when it's supposed to be here?" he grumbled, embarrassment winning out.

"I put it there yesterday after deciding it would be easier for you to find if you got up before I did. Anyway, if you'd checked, you'd have noticed I'd already loaded a packet into the filter."

As he listened to her finish preparing and starting the machine, Ben mentally kicked himself and closed the louvered pantry doors. Brilliant start, he commended himself. He couldn't have reacted more clumsily if he'd tried.

He circled the island, belatedly wondering if the shirt and slacks he'd dressed in clashed or if his hair was combed right. When a man resigned himself to the necessity of doing some fast groveling, the last thing he needed was a cowlick to further humiliate himself.

"I wasn't sure you'd be speaking to me this morning," he mumbled, catching the scent of hyacinth and the undertones of lemon just before he sensed her nearness.

"Neither was I."

He supposed he deserved that. "Did you sleep well?"

"Very."

"Oh. I didn't—in case you're wondering why I look so drawn. I don't think I got two hours all night."

"I'm not surprised."

All right, maybe he deserved that, too, but did she have to sound so cheerful? Feeling wounded and more than a little confused, he followed the sound of her movements as she went to a cabinet to retrieve cups and saucers, and then to pull out what sounded like the electric skillet. That was a hopeful sign—unless she planned to broadside him with it. "I'd like to talk about what happened last night."

"Do you want whole wheat pancakes this morning, French toast or eggs and bacon?"

No hemlock? "Umm . . . eggs and bacon would be wonderful, thank you."

"You're welcome. Now, if you don't mind, go sit down or something. You're in my way."

He scratched his upper lip to hide his smile. This certainly sounded like a reprieve to him. Wanting to stay in her good favor, yet remain as close as possible, Ben took a seat on one of the bar stools at the counter.

"You didn't answer my question," he murmured when it appeared she had nothing more to say to him.

"You didn't ask one, you made a statement."

"I meant I wanted to talk about why I said what I said last night."

"So talk."

Ben's answering laugh was brief. "Jessie, you really know how to make things difficult for a man."

"That's not what you said last night. Last night you suggested I made things very easy for you," she replied, briskly cracking eggs into a dish.

"But I didn't mean—it was never my intention to hurt you."

"Only to push me away again, is that it?"

"Because it was the right thing to do."

"Which was not," Jessie said, dropping something into the frying pan causing it to sizzle, "even remotely close to what you really wanted."

Ben lowered his head and toyed with the fringed edges of a cloth place mat. Just the reminder of what he'd wanted, what he'd felt last night was enough to get his blood heating again. "I take full responsibility for things going as far as they did. Blame it on my condition or being pent up in the hospital for so long—"

"Oh, Ben, for once admit the truth!" Jessie was suddenly beside him. The cup and saucer she placed before him rattled as she set them down. "You're a phony."

"I beg your pardon?"

"You've been lying all these years when you said you weren't attracted to me."

"I never denied that you were an attractive woman."

"I said 'attracted to me,'" she whispered, leaning so close he could feel the caress of her breath against his cheek when she spoke. "Last night proved it. I may not have a lot of experience where men are concerned, but I know when a man's body is speaking to mine. Ben... you were on fire."

His temperature soared another few notches and he had to make a conscious effort to resist sighing in relief when she withdrew and went back to the skillet and turned the bacon. Out of necessity he reached for his cup and took a careful sip of coffee to wet his parched throat. "So I'm human," he muttered.

"In every way that counts."

"Jessie—could we move this conversation along?"

"What would you have me do, forget you ever touched me? Kissed me? Whispered the things you did?"

"Yes!"

"I can't. More importantly I won't."

Feeling a surge of joy and desire flare within him, Ben grimly smashed it down. "You'd better, because it won't happen again."

"If you say so."

"I mean it!"

"You needn't shout."

It was either that or explode from frustration. And how could she be so calm? Here he was about to go up in smoke, but she was acting as if they were discussing nothing more scintillating than their breakfast preferences. He needed her to see reason. He needed her to understand that after one lapse in his resolve, he'd come to his senses and was trying to reestablish acceptable parameters for their relationship.

"What will you say to Marco?" he challenged, confident that would get her to start thinking more levelheadedly.

"Under the circumstances I don't think that's any of your business."

"Under the circumstances, it damn well is," Ben snapped knowing he sounded like a pompous jerk, but for once not caring.

"As you've already pointed out, last night won't be repeated," Jessica said calmly. "And we both know you're a man of your word. So it would really be cruel to say anything to Marco, wouldn't it? As a doctor, he has enough stress in his life. He doesn't need me to add to it."

Ben felt as if he'd taken a blow solidly between the eyes. Had he heard her correctly? "You mean you're still going to go out with him?"

"Of course not. How can I when I'm here with you?"

Fishing wasn't a sport Ben dwelled on, much less participated in, but he knew when he was being fed line. The problem was, he was tempted to run with it anyway.

Despite knowing he would be inviting himself to a future of restless nights, he focused on the most important point she'd just touched upon; the longer she stayed with him, the less vulnerable, not to mention accessible, she would be to Marco. Viewed from that standpoint, it didn't seem he had much choice.

"Ben?"

"Hmm?"

"How do you want your egg?"

"Scrambled," he muttered. "It'll match the condition of my brains."

Jessie laughed softly. "That's the spirit. Just go with the flow."

"Mmm . . . and you can have them embroider that bit of wisdom on my straightjacket."

"Okay, come see what I've done with your clothes."

Ben had been only half listening to one of the taped books Jessie had borrowed for him from the library. When she placed her hand on his shoulder, he found he was relieved to abandon the overzealous Captain Ahab to his hunt for the great white whale. "What did you do?" he asked, having wondered continuously about the sounds he'd heard emanating from his room. "Punch holes numbering the days of the week in my shirt collars?"

"Grump. Are you determined to stay in a bad mood or are you going to try making the most of your days until you regain your eyesight?"

Though he allowed her to draw him from the couch, Ben couldn't resist replying, "Fifty-three nurses at San Antonio General and I get stuck with Little Mary Sunshine."

Jessie led him to the master bedroom and into the walk-in closet. "Give me your hand," she said, sliding hers down the length of his arm and lifting it to the clothes neatly racked. "Now pay attention. Starting from left to right you'll find a shirt and a pair of pants in a coordinating color on each hanger. The shades are separated, too. There are five gray outfits—you know I never realized how much you like that color."

"Liking has nothing to do with it. I grew up hearing my mother always insisting it accented my gray eyes."

"So does blue, so does pink. Blue, by the way, is the next group. See how I've separated then with another hanger and these pieces of cardboard?"

"Aren't you the clever one," he drawled, impressed despite wanting to remain rankled over how much fun she'd had at his expense during breakfast. "Is this a nice way of telling me I'm wearing polka dots with plaid?"

"You're wearing a red shirt and gray pants, which, I might add, look very nice. But I thought you'd worry about the odds of successfully pulling that off every day."

He already had been. Had he relayed that message somehow or was this just another example of how well she had come to know him? "What have you done with my suits?" he asked, struggling to ignore the good feelings her caring gave him.

Jessie directed his hand toward the back of the closet. "I've pushed them out of the way for now. You won't need them until you start back at the office and doing consultations."

"Thank you," he murmured gruffly, deciding not to indulge in his usual cynical response to that kind of optimism. "It's obvious you went to a lot of work."

"Don't mention it." Jessie planted a light kiss on his cheek before reaching across him to switch off the closet light. "Come on, it's time to put you to work."

Ben had difficulty keeping up with what she'd said because he was wondering about what just happened. No, he told himself, it had been an accident that her breast had brushed against his arm. "Work?" he asked finally. "Doing what?"

"You'll see," she replied, already drawing him back down the hall.

It wasn't long before Ben amended his original conclusion. If the contact in his closet was an accident, he was Leonardo Da Vinci, because Jessie got progressively clumsier throughout the day.

"Not there. Here."

When Jessie took Ben's hand and directed it one slot over in the silverware drawer to the forks, he felt a brief tingling as the hairs on his forearms lifted. Was this the sixth or seventh time now? They hadn't even had lunch yet and already he'd lost count of how many times she'd brushed against him, accidentally bumped him or simply, blatantly, used whatever excuse available to touch him.

"I see," he murmured. In more ways than one.

As she withdrew and he counted out two forks to finish setting their places for lunch, Ben decided he'd been wrong to underestimate her potential in this arena. The lady had declared an open season, on him, and one thing was becoming increasingly clear: as resolute as he thought he was at resisting Jessie, she

was proving an admirable adversary in proving him
vulnerable.

After the episode with rearranging his clothes, there
had been phone calls to make to his parents and to his
sister Shelley. Dialing for him hadn't been good
enough this time. No, she'd insisted he learn by touch
himself. With her fingers guiding his, of course.

And then she'd become fascinated with his photo
albums. Fool he'd been to think that was one pastime
she could indulge in without including him. Instead,
she'd joined him on the couch and for forty-five minutes he'd tolerated it. They sat knee to knee as she
paged through one album after another, cooing and
chuckling and generally inflaming him, until he
thought the hair on his head and the soles on his loaf-
ers were smoking.

"Would you like a glass of wine with your salad?"
she asked, drawing him back to the present.

"No, thanks." That was all he needed. Wine and
Jessie. The combination already sounded lethal just
saying it in his mind. "Iced tea will be fine."

"Okay. Have a seat because here come the salads."

Ben slipped onto his bar stool and waited as she approached and set a platter before him. What? he
thought dryly. No little extra pats or strokes?

Then she leaned across him to put her salad in its
place and he was reminded of how taut her belly was
and how slender her waist.

Ben sighed inwardly.

"Excuse me," Jessie murmured.

"No problem."

"Don't forget your napkin."

"I hadn't planned on—"

"Oops," she said, as it was mysteriously plucked out of his fingers. He felt it slip down between his knees to the carpeted floor. "Don't worry, I'll get it."

Ben gritted his teeth together as she used his thigh to steady herself and crouch down to retrieve the linen cloth. "Jessie," he said, his voice sounding thready even to his own ears. "Now and then it really wouldn't hurt to let me start fending for myself."

"Oh, but I enjoy helping you."

"You've made that abundantly clear. But—" He almost groaned as she smoothed the napkin over his lap.

"Good. Because if I slip up or forget anything, I want you to feel free to tell me—whatever it is that disturbs you."

"I have a feeling you'll be the first to know."

"Ma'am . . . sir."

It was mid-afternoon when the police officer who'd stopped by yesterday knocked on the front door.

"Officer Grimes," Jessica said, not quite able to hide the concern in her voice. "What brings you back?"

"Only good news. I wanted to let you both know it's all over. We've caught the man who attacked Dr. Collier. He's in custody and considering his track record and the charges we're about to file against him, I don't think you'll have to worry about his making bail, let alone parole, anytime soon."

"Ben!" Hearing him come up behind her, Jessie spun around and hugged him. "Isn't that wonderful news? It's over."

"Yes, so it seems."

He sounded vague and bemused. Knowing he was experiencing a touch of shock and needed a chance to come to terms with the news, Jessie thanked the policeman and after shutting the door, led Ben back to the living room.

"Sit here," she said, directing him to the couch. She sat right beside him and hugged him again. "I'm so happy I don't know what to say."

"I suppose in the back of my mind, I never really believed they'd get him."

"I know you didn't." She rested her head on his shoulder. All day she'd been mischievous, testing his resistance to her. Now all that was forgotten as she felt the steady beat of his heart against her hand. "This is just the beginning," she whispered, closing her eyes and smiling with relief and gratitude. "Next you'll get your vision back, you'll see."

Ben covered the hand on his chest with his. "Where do you get your strength?"

From love, she wanted to cry. "I just believe in you," she told him instead.

"I don't deserve you." His voice was a rough whisper, as rough as his sigh as he closed his eyes and drew her hand to his lips for a fervent kiss. "If it wasn't for your stubbornness, charming though it is—"

"Some people prefer to call it faith."

"Faith," he amended, beginning to smile.

"Though I liked the 'charming' part."

"Jessie, you're incorrigible. Delightful but relentless."

"You look like you're surviving me pretty well."

"Don't let this stiff upper lip fool you. Right now I feel as though every nerve ending in my body has been rubbed raw with steel wool."

She made a tsking sound and raised her head to gaze at him. "I could kiss you and see if it makes it better?"

"Your judgment seems to have more and more credibility these days," he whispered back, gripping her fingers more tightly.

"Is that a yes?"

"That's a yes... please... and hurry."

But no sooner had he spoken than the phone began to ring. Jessica uttered a disbelieving sound and rushed to answer it. "Hello!" she muttered resentfully.

"Well, this doesn't sound like a woman who's doing handsprings over having our golden boy all to herself."

"Marco." She barely suppressed a groan and glanced over her shoulder in time to watch Ben stiffen. "Hi. What's wrong?"

"Nothing's wrong. I thought I'd keep up illusions and check on you. Don't you think it would arouse the suspicious of our fair-headed friend if I don't keep in touch?"

"Of course. I suppose. I mean I hadn't thought about that."

"My, you sound enthusiastic. I take it he's within hearing distance?"

"Mmm."

"And so if I ask how the great romance of the decade is going, you won't be able to tell me, right?"

"It's good to hear your voice, too."

"Uh-huh...too bad I left my decoder book at home. Well, okay. So are you at least making some headway?"

"Not now I'm not," she muttered, her heart sinking as she saw Ben frown and shift restlessly.

"Why do I get the feeling I should have postponed this call by—oh, say an hour or two?"

"Next time you might want to consider that. But never mind, let me tell you the good news. They've caught the man who attacked Ben. The police just stopped by to tell us."

"Hey, that's great. I'll pass it around."

"We'd appreciate it because I'm fairly certain Ben will be busy phoning his family."

"I like that 'we' business."

"Please behave."

"Okay...you know you two should celebrate."

"Now there's something we can agree on."

"Would you like some helpful hints from an expert?"

"Do you know any that aren't X-rated?" Suddenly Jessica saw Ben rise from the couch. Without comment he headed for his bedroom. "Ben?"

"What's wrong?" Marco asked.

"What do you think is wrong?" she replied in a barely audible whisper. "He left the room. He obviously thinks we need privacy."

"What I wouldn't give to see the expression on his face when he walked out."

"Enough, Marco. Say goodbye because I'm about to hang up and go after him."

"All right, kiddo. I get the message. Give our boy our best and tell him we're happy for the news, which I'll pass along promptly. I'll call you tomorrow."

"I can't wait."

"That's what I thought," he replied laughing. "*Ciao.*"

Jessie hung up and drew her lower lip between her teeth. Of all the rotten timing. Where had Ben gone off to, and what kind of mood would he be in when she found him? Damn, she thought, just when things had been going so well.

She hurried down the hall ready to apologize—not for anything she'd done, because she hadn't done anything. But he'd jumped to conclusions again and she didn't want him slipping back into old patterns.

But once in his bedroom, she heard the sound of water running in his bathroom sink. It appeared he was splashing water over his face. She would bet it was cold water.

A slow smile curved her lips. On second thought she would leave things as they were. Maybe, she told herself as she tiptoed back to the living room, Marco's call had been well-timed after all.

Chapter Eight

"Okay, up off that couch, mister," Jessica called as she marched into the living room with the load of folded towels she'd just removed from the dryer. "Time to get that blood pumping and those muscles flexing."

Ben didn't budge from his prone position, but he did use the remote control to lower the volume on the TV so she would be able to hear his unimpressed reply. "You must be kidding."

She hugged the fluffy, clean-smelling towels to her chest and exhaled dramatically. In the last three days he'd resisted every attempt she'd made to tease him, flirt with him or generally keep him busy and, though she had yet to reach the end of her patience, she was fast running out of ideas.

She knew he wasn't doing this because he liked being a couch potato; on the contrary, she believed the act was harder on him than her. But apparently he'd decided it was the best way to make himself unappealing to her. Little did he know it would take an entirely different type of persuasion to turn her away.

"No, I'm not kidding," she told him cheerfully. "The laundry is done and the kitchen's as tidy as your housekeeper left it. I thought now would be a good time, not to mention fun, to take a walk around the block and get some fresh air."

Though he turned off the set completely, Ben shook his head. "Thanks, I'll pass. Being stared at by a bunch of housewives who are bored and have nothing else to do while they're waiting for their favorite soap opera to come on TV is not my idea of a fun time."

"Mrs. Friedlander is a widow and she likes game shows not the soaps. Anyway, one lonely old lady confessing she watched you and I go to the mailbox while she was dusting her mini-blinds does not constitute a Peeping Tom epidemic."

"I'm not going. They just announced it's already ninety degrees outside."

"You can wear a hat and your sunglasses."

"I don't own any hats."

Narrowing her eyes with intent, Jessica crossed over to him and dropped her bundle of neatly folded towels on his belly. "Oops—how clumsy of me," she drawled.

"Hey!" Ben sat up and grabbed at the scattering deluge. "Jessie, one more 'oops' out of you and— these were already folded."

"Isn't that a shame. No matter. You can help me refold them. It'll allow you to earn your keep around here."

Unable to hide his amusement completely, Ben allowed one corner of his mouth to curve upward. "You think you're being cute, don't you?"

"And clever. But it's such exhausting work." Sitting on the coffee table so her knees touched his, she took a blue-and-green striped bath towel and began refolding it. "The only thing that keeps me going is my determination to show you I'm more stubborn than you are."

"Really? Now you're accusing me of being out to prove something?"

"Let's say that it doesn't matter how unpleasant and unsociable you attempt to be, I've met the *real* Ben Collier, and he's the reason I'm determined to wait out this grouch who's invaded his body."

Ben scowled and for a moment looked as though he might dump the whole pile of towels on the couch and walk out on her. Instead, he picked up a towel himself and concentrated on refolding it. "It's just that I'm fed up with this blindness, Jessie," he muttered at last.

"I know you are. But tomorrow you're scheduled for a checkup. Maybe we'll hear some good news. In the meantime, why not try to be glad that otherwise you have your health and that your strength is returning more and more with each passing day."

"Must every cloud have a silver lining with you?"

"When they're hovering over *your* head, yes. Listen, I have an idea . . . why don't we go celebrate properly?"

"You know how I feel about crowds."

"Wait. Hear me out, please," she said, touching his hand. "I could make us some sandwiches or something and we could take one of those pedal boats through the canals down at the River Walk."

"Good grief. Talk about public places...why don't we spread out a blanket on the steps of city hall already?"

"Stop exaggerating. It wouldn't be that bad. There are quieter spots to explore, places away from Rivercenter and all the restaurants, hotels and shops. I remember one that's particularly pretty, like a tropical lagoon."

"Someplace you've explored before with another—friend?"

"No." She ignored the little jig her heart did at the thought he might be jealous. "By myself. While I was in training I would go there to study and sometimes just sit, feed the birds. Please, Ben? The pedaling would be good exercise for you."

He uttered a deep growl of frustration and added the last of the towels to the top of the folded ones on her lap. "Why do I let you wrap me around your finger like this?"

"*Are* you?" she asked, pretending amazement. "I hadn't noticed."

"You know you'll end up getting your way. The question is, what's my reasoning for allowing it?"

"Because you usually like the end results."

She watched his expression go from frustrated to startled, then more reluctantly to amused and, yes, there was even an unmistakable hint of desire. "Anyone ever tell you that you have the stamina of a terrier pup?"

"If you want to call me a pain in the neck," she murmured, her gaze roaming adoringly over his face, "you're going to have to do it without anyone else's endorsement."

Instead he drew in a slow, deep breath, his nostrils flaring with the effort. As she watched him wrestle with some inner demon, Jessica felt her own body tingle with excitement. Amazing, she thought. He wasn't even touching her and yet she felt as though he was, intimately.

"Should I change?" he asked gruffly.

Jessie considered his light blue shirt and gray pants. "No need," she murmured. "You're perfect."

"No." With impressive accuracy, Ben reached out and stroked her hair. "That's where your vision's myopic. And I'm afraid that one of these days you're going to figure that out."

Jessie insisted they use her car and she parked at it one of the lots near *La Villita* adjacent to the River Walk. She guided Ben through the collection of restored cabins and cottages that now housed artists and craftsmen. As she held Ben's arm, she could feel his tension and wariness, though behind his sunglasses, his face seemed the picture of composure.

"Watch these stone steps," she warned, adjusting the tote bag on her shoulder that served as both purse and picnic carrier.

"Great. If memory serves, there's only about a thousand and sixty of the damned things."

His droll tone didn't fool her. He might be anxious about making a spectacle of himself, but he'd also taken several vigorous breaths of fresh air since they'd left his condominium and Jessie guessed he wasn't completely unhappy about being outdoors.

"Nah, no more than forty or fifty," she replied good-naturedly. "Anyway, it's all downhill. Even at your age that shouldn't present much of a problem."

"Watch it, wise guy. Many more remarks like that and you'd better have worn your running shoes."

"Empty threats," she dismissed airily.

"You hope."

"I have them on. I can always dare you."

Thrilled that he was beginning to play along with her, she eased him out of the way of several pedestrians coming up the steps. Seconds later there was a wolf whistle behind them. Ben's contented expression turned into a stony mask of annoyance.

"I take it that wasn't for me," he said, stiffly.

"Well, you were being sized up by an attractive brunette when we started down the stairs, but she looked more like the type to slip you her business card. No, those were a few servicemen. Apparently some of the boys from one of the air bases have leave and they're out sightseeing."

"Young barbarians."

"They were just admiring my legs, Ben. If you remember correctly, they aren't half bad looking."

"I'm only blind, not senile." After descending a few more steps he added, "What are you wearing?"

"Shorts...white ones...and a red T-shirt. Regular tourist garb, but quite respectable."

"I'll bet. We're not even down to where most of the traffic is and you've already been propositioned."

"Hardly."

"Ogled then." They descended several more steps. "Maybe you should have worn one of those sundress things."

"For a ride on a pedal boat? Not very practical."

"Well, there's always slacks."

"Too hot."

"*I'm* wearing them."

Jessica grinned, enjoying herself immensely. "That's different. I was going to suggest you change into something cooler before we left, but I didn't want to embarrass you because I knew how pale your legs had gotten since you've been hiding indoors."

"I have not been hiding, I've been recuperating."

"Whatever." They'd reached the bottom of the steps and Jessica hugged his arm, brimming with happiness. "It's not crowded at all today, Ben. And it's so pretty. Like a postcard an Impressionist might have painted. Someday I want to come down here in the evening when all the trees' lights are lit along with the candles on all these restaurant tables. I'll bet it's romantic."

"Hasn't Marco taken you down here?" Ben asked casually. "I thought it was one of his favorite haunts, too," When she didn't answer, he grimaced. "I'm sorry. That was pretty transparent, wasn't it?"

"Yes, it was."

Ben lowered his head. "Could we start over? Pretend we're simply two friends sharing a pleasant few hours?"

I don't have to pretend, Jessica told him with her eyes. But when she spoke she replied, "I'd like that."

She was, Ben discovered, an excellent guide as well as being wonderful company. He may not have initially wanted to go on this outing, but she soon had him so thoroughly caught up in her vivacity as she described their surroundings that he all but forgot that.

"Oh, Ben, quick! Stop pedaling."

"What's wrong?"

"Ducks."

"Good grief, did we run over one?"

"No, silly, I want to feed them some of this bread I brought from home."

Ben told himself it was foolish to feel such a rush of pleasure over her using a simple word like *home,* but he did. "I thought you might have fed it all to the mass of pigeons that attacked us at that bridge we went under a few minutes ago."

"I brought plenty."

"Translate that to mean she brought it all," he said to the world at large. But he smiled as he lifted his arm off the back of her seat and toyed with the curls that had been temptingly brushing against his skin. "Tomorrow morning you'll be serving me saltines instead of toast with breakfast."

"Hmm . . . come to think of it, maybe we'd better stop at the market on our way home."

Dear heaven he wanted that—not just *one* trip to a market with her but dozens, thousands. And he wanted that many breakfasts and dinners, plus countless lazy evenings when they would snuggle together on the same couch. He would glance over from one of his journals and see if she'd gotten to a steamy love scene in one of her romance novels, and then show her how a woman should really be loved.

Ben was so caught up in the wanting, visualizing the dream, that it took him a moment to realize he was actually looking at Jessie's profile. Well, almost, he amended, blinking. It was more like looking at her through a foggy photo lens, but his heart began to pound anyway because this was the sharpest his vision had been yet.

He almost told her. He'd already parted his lips to speak, felt the tingling in fingers that yearned to grab her and crush her to him. But he caught himself just in time.

Wait and see how long it lasts, he warned himself. As with his last experience, it might only be temporary. Besides, Jessie would insist they go to the hospital for a complete checkup. He preferred this, sharing the moment with her even though she was unaware of what was happening to him.

"Now that you're finished," he said when she retied the bread bag, "why don't we find that spot you were describing earlier? I'm getting hungry."

He caught her startled movement. "How did you know I'd finished feeding?"

Behind his sunglasses, Ben closed his eyes and be-
rated himself for nearly giving himself away. "The
little beggars are squawking again and I can't hear
their bills attacking the water the way they had been."

"Oh. For a moment— I mean, that's very good."

Ben could tell she had to work at hiding her disappointment from him and for a moment he felt guilty.
But better guilty than premature, he reassured himself.

"What's for lunch?" he asked gently.

"I decided on an assortment of crackers, cheese and
fruit."

"That's *it?* After all this pedaling?"

"I'm planning to make a big dinner once we get
home."

"I'll never survive," he groaned, though a satisfied
smile soon followed because she'd said that one word
again.

They pedaled onward. Ben took a secret pleasure in
being able to identify the lush boughs arcing over-
head and, every now and then, the brightest of the
flowers adorning hotel balconies, store entrances and
windowsills.

"The first time I saw this place I remember telling
my mother I was going to live here when I grew up so
I could have a bedroom with a balcony overlooking
the canals," Jessie said dreamily. "I had it all figured
out. I was going to be a court stenographer or maybe
a beautician so I could treat her to weekly wash-and-
sets. Did I ever tell you she had the most glorious
hair?"

"So do you."

"Not like Mama's. Anyway, by night I was going to sit on my balcony filling my diary with all the fascinating adventures I'd had during the day. Until one evening I'd look down at the people strolling by and I would see him."

"Him?"

"*Him.* He'd be sitting at the café on the other side of the canal, sketching furiously as he tried to capture the way the moonlight shimmered on my hair and on my skin."

"Ah. Did he do you justice?"

"Oh, yes. Eventually he would do a version in oils and it would make the cover of *Time.*"

"I'm impressed."

"That's not all. Willie Nelson would buy the original charcoal sketch at an auction."

"Willie Nelson?"

"Try to remember I was a mere child. Anyway, I adored his music... the whole country and western sound. Still do. In my room I had this reversible poster. On one side was a black-and-white ink drawing of Mozart— I always turned it that side out when I went to school, just in case Aunt Evelyn came into my room—and on the other was Willie in his braids and bandanna."

"You do have eclectic tastes, don't you?"

"Well, think about it... There's so many different types and styles for so many different things. Why should we be forced to choose one over the other simply because they happen to contradict each other?"

"I can't really say I've given it a lot of thought."

"Sure you did. You had to when you decorated your home. You took a conservative approach."

"Because I'm a conservative guy."

"But your bedroom suggests otherwise," she countered. "See what I mean? Now I think that if someone had a house decorated with antiques and they wanted to hang a modern print on the wall, they should do it. Or how about if they're more emotionally driven as I am? I'd hate to have to look at a place day in and day out that only soothed or stimulated one side of me."

"I think I'm beginning to see your point—good grief, there's a dangerous concept."

"Make fun if you like, but I think that old saying about variety being the spice of life holds a lot of merit," she said with a shrug. Then she gave an excited little gasp and steered toward the bank. "We're here."

"At last," Ben drawled. "I was beginning to lose hope that we'd make land before nightfall."

"No sea legs, huh? Stay put while I secure this thing to this post."

Ben waited for her to leap to land, admiring her grace, but more, her lithe figure. When she told him to give her his hand, he did so, careful to aim just to the right of her. When he jumped, he made it seem accidental that he overreached and had to grab her waist to keep her from falling backward.

"Did I hurt you?" he asked, ignoring the inner voice that warned him he was behaving with dangerous irrationality. But his less rational side rebelled; he was regaining his *sight.* He couldn't be expected to fully contain his euphoria.

"No. Are you all right? Your face is quite flushed."

"Are you kidding? If Balboa would have kept this pace when he crossed the isthmus of Panama, he'd have given up before he even got out of the city limits of Cristobah."

"City limits of..." Jessie burst into delighted laughter. "Come on you," she said, taking his arm and leading him farther inland. "Now I *know* you need to rest. You're beginning to sound as crazy as me!"

She led him several yards to what she described as a series of stone steps half overgrown with grass. On either side of them were stone-encased flower beds where fern, pink, white and red impatiens, black-eyed Susans and daisies bloomed in semi-wild profusion.

When they sat down, she opened her tote bag and drew out a thermos of iced mineral water and the meticulously wrapped packages of cheese, fruit and crackers. Jessie's idea of eating a picnic lunch, Ben soon realized, was for her to keep all the goodies out of his reach, and for her to hand-feed him.

"You're spoiling me," he warned as he swallowed another bite of cracker adorned with Brie and a sliver of pear.

"It's the least I can do since you've been such a good sport about this. You *are* happy you came, aren't you, Ben?"

"Do you really have to ask?" His smile was whimsical. "Have you noticed you've stopped calling me

Doc? I wonder what our resident shrinks would have
to say about that?''

"Probably that I don't have the sense of a kiwi. But
I've resigned myself to that. I wouldn't have missed
the last few days for anything.''

"Why?''

"Because you've let me see a side of you that otherwise I might never have known.''

With a self-deprecating laugh Ben concentrated on
shredding the daisy he'd blindly sought and plucked.
"What a treat, considering that most of the time I've
been rotten to everyone who came near me.''

"No— I don't mean the front you put on to try to
keep us, especially me, at a distance. I mean the moments when you let me see the man beneath.''

He lifted his head, his expression grateful that she
could recall those. "There've been one or two, haven't
there?''

"That's what makes them special.''

Ben searched for and found another flower, this
time, he noted from its size and raised center, a black-
eyed Susan. After twirling it in his fingers, he sighed
and offered it to her. "Jessie…how am I supposed to
resist you when you say things like that?''

"Oh, you'll do just fine,'' she replied, her voice
echoing the sadness she'd heard in his. "You usually
do manage.''

He closed his eyes to avoid the temptation of trying
to search her face. How he'd hurt her. He could feel it
and it was more than he could bear. In trying to protect her from himself, he'd slowly been stifling the very
qualities he cherished in her. He was tired of it; he was

tired of fighting his own common sense. How smart was he, if in denying himself, he made her miserable?

He sighed. "Let's not dwell on the past any longer," he murmured, carefully seeking and finding her. He slipped his hand behind her head and drew her toward him. "Let's— Ah, Jessie, I just want this."

He brought her lips to his, savoring her warmth. Excitement...hunger...heat...built quickly, until he felt it throb inside him. No one had ever tempted him to lose control like Jessie. He didn't know whether he was grateful or resentful that they were in a public place where any moment someone could pass by; he only knew he needed to sate some of the need churning within him.

At the sound of her own trembly sigh, he deepened the kiss. She tasted of the peach she'd just eaten.

"Ben," Jessie whispered, the sound both a question and an entreaty.

"More." The word was a prayer uttered against her lips as he drew her closer so that her small, firm breasts were pressed tightly against the erratic beat of his heart.

Yes, this was what he wanted. As he held her close, her arms looped around his shoulders, her hands unsteady but eagerly exploring the cords of his neck. His own were busy offering encouragement, relaxing her, slowly massaging away the lingering tension he felt in her back. She'd come to expect rejection from him. It hurt to think he'd taught her that. And so he set out to teach her trust.

Her smallness intrigued and delighted him. As he expanded his exploration, his widely splayed fingers inched outward until the sweeping, circular strokes brushed the outside swells of her breasts. The delicious, breathless moan she made had him repeating the caress again, and then again.

"I've dreamed of doing this." He nuzzled her cheek to catch his own breath. "Touching you here."

"I didn't know."

"I tried to deny it. As usual."

"It feels wonderful."

"*You* feel wonderful." He kissed her temple and her chin, then her lips because he couldn't resist them for more than seconds at a time. "Soft...sleek...do you know what it feels like to have your nipples tightening against me like this?"

Instead of answering, she made a tortured sound and buried her face against his shoulder.

"Don't hide from me," he said with a groan. "I don't mean to embarrass you."

"I'm not embarrassed. I'm just— I'm afraid you'll stop."

"Oh, sweet heaven . . . Jessie, let me have your mouth." The instant he felt her begin to raise her head, he ducked his and crushed his lips to hers.

This next kiss was rapacious, darker and explosive. Soon their breathing was reduced to shallow gasps and exploration centered on the intimate glide of his tongue over hers. Hers over his. Possession. It had Ben experiencing a sensation not unlike being part of a flood rushing over the top of a dam. He raced a series of torrid kisses down Jessie's throat all the way to the V of her T-shirt.

"I want to do this to every inch of you," he whispered against her fragrant skin. "Hold your breasts in my hands . . . taste you."

The images that spawned pushed Ben's ardor beyond any point of rational thought. Unable to resist his desire, he sat up and drew her onto his lap, needing her closer, wanting her to understand the full extent of his desire.

"Ben . . . I want you. I want you so much it hurts," Jessie whispered between his incendiary kisses.

"*Yes.*" The hissed word was an echo of his own pain.

It was the giggles of two young boys running past that brought them back to sanity. Jessie stiffened. If Ben hadn't had a firm hold of her, she would probably have bolted out of his arms. He accepted that he'd almost carried things too far, but he wasn't yet willing to see the moment end. Tightening his arms, he prolonged it by stroking her hair and rocking her soothingly.

"We did nothing to be ashamed of," he insisted, when she remained rigid.

"No, but we should really be heading back."

"In a minute."

"Let me go, Ben. I hated that—being laughed at."

"They were kids, Jessie. You know how boys are at a certain age. In a couple years they'll be wishing they were in my place."

"Thanks a lot."

Ben grimaced. "I meant that as a compliment. Jessie, sweetheart, no man could look at you and not feel a little envious of whoever you were with."

This time she did succeed in freeing herself. "I don't want to be wanted because of some macho ego thing. I want to be wanted for *me*."

She was right. She deserved better than what she'd received at his hands. As she turned away from him, reached for her tote bag and began clearing up their lunch things, Ben covertly watched her.

What a mess of mixed signals he'd been giving her. It was about time he faced the truth that he loved her, had loved her for a long time. The reasons he'd used to resist her—except for his sight, which clearly seemed to be returning—were, suddenly, so empty and trivial.

Still one big problem remained. Marco.

"Let me help you to the pedal boat," Jessie said, breaking into his thoughts.

Ben let her, deciding it would be better to give her something else to focus on right now. He needed to think—and plan. Number one on his list was having a serious talk with Marco.

Jessie chewed on her lower lip until it was raw. Though the ride back seemed to go quickly enough, Ben had barely said a dozen words to her. But then she wasn't exactly bubbling over with conversation herself.

He didn't look angry; he looked more preoccupied. What was he thinking about? Was he sorry he'd kissed her again? She didn't think so, but then why wasn't he talking to her?

You should be the one talking.

Yes, she decided firmly. Before another day passed, she needed to tell him the truth about Marco, explain what she'd done and why. Things had definitely changed between them, in which case maybe he wouldn't take the news as badly as she'd first thought he would.

As they approached the spot where they would turn in the boat, Jessie concentrated on steering. There were two boats ahead of them and one behind. She eased her craft into its slot and waited for the handler to secure them. Then she accepted his hand and jumped to land.

"Okay, Ben," she said, leaning back to reach for his arm. "We're here. Give me your hand."

She hadn't noticed that the two teenage girls in back had been having problems trying to maneuver in behind them until it was too late. Ben had only lifted a foot toward land when the girls' boat struck the back of theirs. Propelled backward he was wrenched from Jessie's grasp.

It seemed to happen in slow motion. One moment he seemed to recover, the next he was falling backward into the path of an oncoming tourist barge.

Jessie screamed in terror.

Chapter Nine

"Ben! Oh, God—" Jessica jumped back onto the pedal boat and grabbed for him as he struggled to stay afloat and get his bearings. "Ben, I'm here! Come toward my voice. Reach for me. I'll help you in."

She shot a worried look at the barge crammed with tourists sitting along the bench seats, voicing their own dismay and concern. But to her relief the pilot was slowing down and pulling over to the far side of the canal. Satisfied that one danger had been neutralized, she refocused on Ben.

"Got you!" she cried, grabbing his outstretched arm. She pulled him toward her, too upset to find it amusing or even ironic that his sunglasses had only gone slightly askew in the fall.

When she could, she used her other hand to take hold of his belt and gave a mighty tug. Though he groaned in pain, Ben finished hoisting himself up onto the pedal boat.

The floorboard proved cramped enough for one person, let alone two, so as quickly as she could catch her breath, and relying on the attendant for balance, she eased herself back onto land. Then she coaxed Ben to follow.

Once they were both safe, and indifferent to the water pouring off him—and to the audience they'd involuntarily collected—Jessie wrapped her arms around his waist and buried her face against his shoulder. "Thank goodness that barge stopped. If the pilot had been less attentive... I don't even want to think what could have happened to you."

"I—I heard it coming," Ben wheezed.

"Are you all right?"

"I think so. Mmph... Jess, honey, watch those ribs."

"Sorry." Minutes ago she'd been in his arms like this and her only thoughts had been of wanting him to keep kissing her. Now she had to push that interlude, and all romantic thought, to the back of her mind and concentrate on his well-being. She eased her hold to run her hands over his chest, his shoulders, his arms. "Are you sure you're all right? Ben—" she cried when she saw the cut on his right temple "—you're bleeding!"

"I am?" He lifted his hand and touched the already swelling spot on his forehead, bringing away fingers that were tipped in scarlet. "I guess I am. I must have struck something as I fell, but I don't really remember."

From behind her she heard someone say they would phone for an ambulance. Someone else announced they knew where they could find a first-aid kit.

"That would be great, thank you," Jessica tossed over her shoulder. "I'm a nurse. Would everyone please stand back and give us room. Ben," she said, lowering her voice to something more consoling than assertive, "let me get you to a bench a few feet from here and I'll try to stop the bleeding."

Readjusting his glasses, he allowed her to do that, but firmly replied, "I'm not going to any hospital."

Jessica sat down beside him and immediately dug into the tote she'd snatched up for a clean tissue or napkin. "Are you sure you weren't injured anywhere else? I think maybe you reinjured your ribs again."

"No. And that's why I'm not going to the hospital."

"I heard you the first time." She carefully dabbed at the smear of blood on his forehead. "I understand your reluctance and this doesn't look serious, but don't you think it might be best to make sure?"

"I *am* sure."

"Nevertheless, you're going."

"Not in any ambulance, I'm not."

"Of all the headstrong—" She broke off and gave a sigh of resignation. "All right. We'll go in my car. Is that more agreeable to you?"

"It depends if that's your final offer."

His teasing had her breaking into a reluctant smile and shaking her head as she called over her shoulder, "Cancel the ambulance!"

The man with the first-aid kit arrived and Jessica finished tending to Ben as best she could. After returning the kit to the man, she gave Ben's hand a gentle squeeze. "Do you think you're ready to walk to the car?"

He uttered a brief, dry laugh. "Jessie, I'd crawl on all fours if it meant I could stop feeling as if I was performing center ring in a three-ring circus."

"Then on your feet, party animal, and let's see if we can get there without any more catastrophes."

The trip to the hospital took only a few minutes. When they arrived, Jessica parked by the Emergency entrance and, wrapping a supporting arm around Ben's waist, assisted him inside.

It appeared things were relatively quiet, which was the norm for this hour of the day when the weather was good. Not for the first time did she remind herself that emergencies often seemed to occur in peak traffic hours, at night and in severe weather.

But she soon spotted something else that gave her a jolt. They had barely gotten halfway through the main reception area when she saw Marco and Tanya near the elevators. She froze in midstep. It wasn't only seeing them together that had her eyes widening; it was seeing how they were standing, holding hands and gazing into each other's eyes. Jessica figured the hospital could be sinking in one of those mysterious sinkholes and those two wouldn't have noticed.

She was so preoccupied with them, she never noticed that Ben had stopped at the same instant she did.

"Oh, Marco..." Jessica moaned.

"Marco, for heaven's sake!" Ben snapped.

Jessica shot Ben an incredulous look. How could he have noticed— *He could see?*

"What the devil do you think you're doing?" Ben continued, oblivious to her inspection as he scowled across the room.

"Ben . . . Jessie." Marco's smile of recognition wavered and, murmuring something to Tanya, he hurried over. "What on earth happened to you two? Ben, you're hurt!"

"Never mind me. What I want to know is why you're being such a fool? Don't you realize that by flirting with Tanya, you'll lose Jessica? It is Tanya, isn't it?" he asked more politely. "I'm guessing by Jessie's description of you."

Tanya nodded her head dazedly. "You mean you can *see?*"

"That's exactly *my* question," Jessica said, stunned.

Marco gave them both droll looks. "Isn't it obvious?"

"It must have happened when you fell." Jessica didn't know whether to laugh or cry. Only Ben's guilty expression had her refraining from either impulse. "It did, didn't it?"

"Not exactly. It's been evolving for a while now. But that's not what's important right now. Do you see what your so-called boyfriend is up to while you've been busy taking care of me?"

Rather than answer that, Jessica narrowed her eyes. "Define 'a while.'"

"What difference does it make how long it's been?"

"You'd be surprised," Jessica drawled. She could feel anger and indignation rising inside her. "Did you regain your vision while I was staying with you in your home? You did, I can see you did."

"Jessie, it's not as if it's even twenty-twenty yet . . . and when it started it would come and go."

"Before or after my bubble bath?"

"Bubble bath?" Marco's face brightened with interest before he attempted to cover it with an indignant look. "Would you like to tell me what he's talking about, Jessie?"

Jessica uttered a deep growl between her clenched teeth and shot him a look of warning.

"If you'll just let me explain," Ben said, reaching for her.

She stepped away from him. "Explain? You couldn't say anything that would justify what you did. Didn't you ever consider how concerned I was for you? I was worried *sick.*" She momentarily bit her lip to suppress the quaver in her voice. "This is unbelievable. Knowing how I feel about you—"

"Whoa...hold on right there," Marco injected, his hands going to his hips. "Jessie, what are you talking about? You're supposed to be in love with *me.*"

Behind him, Tanya gasped. "Marco, what are *you* talking about? You just told me that was all an act."

"What do you mean, an act?" Ben demanded.

"Oh, dear." Tanya winced, shooting Marco and Jessica a look of apology. "They thought it might be a good way to snap you out of your depression."

"For heaven's sake, Marco." Jessica moaned. "Isn't there anyone left who doesn't know about this?"

"I had to tell Tanya," he said in self-defense. "She was chewing me out for trying to two-time you when I asked her out. Hey, Jessie, you'll never believe this—Tanya's mother is half Irish. Isn't that great?"

"Wait a minute." Ben glared from his colleague to Jessica. "Are you saying that you two aren't dating each other?"

"Uh—listen, old man," Marco said amiably, trying to calm his friend's ire. "Why don't we check out that cut on your head and then we can all discuss this like civilized adults."

Ben shrugged off the hand Marco placed on his shoulder. "You think it was adult to pretend you and Jessie were—were—?"

"Good friends?" Marco suggested, then shrugged when Tanya shot him a pointed look.

"Of all the childish stupid pranks," Ben snapped.

Crushed that he couldn't see why they'd done it and tired of everything, Jessica lost the last of her patience. "You're absolutely right, Dr. Collier. It was *stupid* to care, to try to show you how much you would be missed if you gave up on yourself, how much you would be missing." Her voice broke and she hastily cleared it. "But most of all it was stupid of me to want you to love me. Anyone with an ounce of intelligence would realize you don't deserve me!"

"Stop right there, pal."

Marco's grip on his arm was firm but, even so,

Ben's intention was to keep walking. Already the automatic sliding glass doors were closing behind Jessie. He needed to stop her before she reached her car.

"Let me go, Marco."

"Soon. We're going to check out that wound on your forehead first."

"Damn it, I told you it was only a scratch. I'll see to it later." After he caught up with Jessie, Ben thought. After he wrung her pretty neck for pulling this stunt and putting him through seven different kinds of torment. After he thanked heaven that none of it was true.

"But we also need to have Wescott take a look at your eyes, Ben."

"My eyes are fine!" But as he again attempted to free himself, a slight touch of vertigo had him wavering on his feet.

Marco adjusted his hold and turned Ben away from the doors. "I'm sure they are, but we're going to take a few minutes to make certain of that. Considering the way Jessie stormed out of here, I have a feeling that knowing when to duck might come in handy." At Ben's chilly glare, he shrugged. "All right, so say it's for insurance purposes. Either way let's call down Wescott. Then we'll get you out of here. You have my word."

"And we all know what that's worth." Ben was pleased to note that at least the younger man had the grace to look embarrassed.

"I suppose I deserved that. Then let's just say Jessie needs time to cool off."

"*She* needs time," Ben muttered, though he let Tanya take his other arm and gently lead him toward one of the examination rooms.

"Dr. Collier," Tanya said softly. "I'm sorry you're so upset, but if only you'd let Marco explain why he and Jessie did what they did, you would probably change your perspective. They had only your welfare in mind. Marco told me that Jessie was beside herself when you were first brought in here after the attack. Later, when everyone realized that you were thwarting your own ability to recuperate, he used his knowledge of Jessie's feelings for you to convince her to visit you."

"And don't think she didn't resist," Marco told him, as Tanya helped Ben onto an examination table. "In fact I really had to push to get her to see you, Ben. Apparently, her last experience in that arena hurt her so deeply, she wasn't willing to risk exposing her feelings to you again."

"Are you suggesting that's why you made up the story about being involved with her?"

"*I* didn't do that, she did."

"Jessie would never do something like that."

"It's your own fault. You scared the hell out of her. If you hadn't growled like a wounded lion ready to toss her out of your room, she wouldn't have panicked and used the first excuse she could think of to convince you she didn't care about you any more."

Ben considered that. "So you weren't dating?"

"Nope."

"Then explain why Nurse Scott said she saw you kiss her."

"Well, I did do it—but purely as a tactical maneuver to stimulate gossip—and before you take a swing at me, let me tell you it wasn't successful. Though if it will make you feel any better, Jessie almost took a swing at me herself when I did it." Marco put his arm around Tanya's waist. "This is the lovely lady I'm really chasing."

"Marco..." Tanya shook her head, but blushed delightfully. "I'd better go phone for Dr. Wescott."

As she left the room, Ben closed his eyes and sighed. "Hell, what a mess."

"But not irreparable," Marco said philosophically, as he leaned close to inspect the wound on Ben's forehead.

"I suppose you know why I pretended to still be blind?"

"Yeah, the same reason you got Jessie to take leave and stay at your place. You were eaten up with jealousy."

"I tried to convince myself it was simply friendly concern. Her family's all gone now...she really has no one."

"Fascinating. You don't, however, strike me as the big brother type."

"It didn't take me long to realize it didn't sit well with me either. And lately I've also come to understand how wrong I was to let the age thing and our personality differences come between us."

"You told her she was too young for you?"

"Twelve years is practically a generation what with the rapid way things seem to be changing these days."

"Let's hear it for progress," Marco cheered. "Have you seen some of the bathing suit styles that are on the beaches this season? Va-va-va-voom."

Ben stared at him without blinking. "Does Tanya know you're an incurable sex maniac?"

"Don't let her shy exterior fool you. My lady and I communicate very well. Anyway, we're supposed to be concentrating on your problem—not that you really have one if you've finally realized Jessie's the best thing that's ever happened to you."

"I thought when I did marry it would be with someone who was reserved and on the serious side, as I am."

Marco let his head drop and pretended to snore.

"Yeah, I suppose you're right," Ben said with a rueful smile. "I didn't realize that differences can be a positive thing. She's forced me to look at it from a new perspective. She's taught me to laugh more—especially at myself."

"That does it. I'm sending her a bottle of my private stock of Pouilly-Fuisée as soon as we're through here."

Ben glanced at him from under his brows. "You think I've been a jerk, don't you?"

"The question is, what are you going to do now?"

"Grovel." Again, he thought with another sigh.

"Might I suggest flowers and a piece of jewelry? Nothing cuts through arctic freezes like diamonds."

Ben slowly, finally began to smile. "I'll take that into consideration." Then, as Marco turned toward the cabinet where supplies were kept, Ben touched his arm and offered his hand in friendship. "I know this is long overdue, but thanks."

It was almost two hours later when Ben emerged from the passenger side of Marco's car and walked up the front steps of his condominium. The cut on his head was covered with a new bandage and his vision, which had been progressively clearing all morning, was now almost normal. After changing into the extra set of clothes he kept in his locker, he'd been ready to jump in a cab and go home, but Marco insisted on driving him there.

Now both men stood at the entrance as Ben dug out his extra key from his wallet and unlocked the door. Since he didn't have his remote control, he couldn't check to see if Jessie's car was still in the garage.

"Jessie?" he called when he stepped into the hallway. "I'm home."

There was no reply and Marco cleared his throat self-consciously. "Maybe she didn't come straight here. Maybe she decided to drive around a bit to sort things out in her own mind."

"Let me check the guest room." Ben went down the hall, every muscle in his body tensing in preparation for disappointment.

The bedroom looked as neat and unoccupied as the day he'd brought her here. Even though he'd half expected this, a feeling of panic began to build in his stomach. Without comment, he strode to the closet and jerked open the door. No suitcase. And the clothes that had been hanging on the racks were missing, too.

"Uh, oh." Marco murmured. "Looks like she means business this time."

"But she didn't even give me a chance to explain."

"She doesn't want to be lectured to anymore by the kindly doctor, Ben. She wants someone to romance her and love her, and treat her like a woman and an equal."

"We were getting around to that," Ben muttered. His gaze fell on the phone on the bedside table and he walked over to it. "Maybe she's back at the hospital looking for me."

He dialed, but a minute later, after learning she hadn't returned, he hung up. Her apartment, he thought, redialing. The phone rang and rang but to no avail.

Behind him, Marco shifted uncomfortably. "Ben, I hate to do this to you, but I have to get back to the hospital."

"Yes...all right. Thanks for the ride."

"Are you sure you're going to be okay? I could try to come back later after my last appointment."

"No, no. There's no need." Thanking him again, Ben walked Marco to the front door.

As soon as he closed it, Ben's expression settled into a worried frown. Where could she have gone? How, after all they'd shared earlier today, could she shut him out like this? He wanted, *needed* one more chance. Already he noticed how empty the condominium seemed without her there.

Unbearably so.

Chapter Ten

Jessica slept in troubled spurts throughout the night. When she awoke the next morning, she felt worse than when she'd caught the flu last winter; her body was one progressive ache from her neck to her toes and she was sure someone had stuffed her head with cotton balls during one of her ten-minute lapses of consciousness. She was half-tempted to bury her head under her pillow and try again, but then she reminded herself that she'd phoned in to her supervisor yesterday afternoon and told her she was once again available to work. A glance at her alarm clock disclosed she had exactly forty-five minutes to get herself presentable and drive to the hospital. With a groan, she pushed herself out of bed.

She had five minutes to spare when she pulled into the employee parking lot. A shower and a strong cup of herb tea had helped her pull herself together. On the outside she knew she looked near normal. She only wished her nerves were in half as good shape.

She cast a wary glance around her looking for the blue BMW that would have had her doing an about-face and returning to her car. Ben wasn't supposed to be here; he wasn't ready for the physical demands of work again. But the way the phone had rung and rung last night—until she'd finally been compelled to pull the jack out of the wall—she wouldn't have been surprised if he'd decided to show up anyway. She'd half expected him to come to her apartment. But he hadn't, and neither was he here.

With her tote bag and purse slung over her shoulder, she hurried across the parking lot, where a construction crew was already busily at work setting several more poles for security lights. She did her best to ignore them as she did the day, which was undoubtedly going to be a carbon copy of yesterday with the sun radiant and only a smattering of puffy clouds marring the eye-tearing brilliance of the sky. Even as she approached the staff entrance, she ducked her head to avoid looking at the beds of impatiens that lined the walkway. It was going to be bad enough getting through today with all the questions she was going to have to face. She didn't want the added reminders of what could have, no, what *should* have been.

Ben. She couldn't even think about him without feeling a knifelike pain shoot through her heart. But this time, she reassured herself, she was going to get him out of her system once and for all. She'd already spent too many years hoping and dreaming for him to wake up and see her standing there waiting for him. It was time to face reality and get on with the rest of her life.

"You can do it," she muttered under her breath as she dialed the correct combination for the lock on her locker. "All you need to remember is that it's one hour at a time and then one day after another."

"Jessie? Have you taken up talking to yourself or are you listening to a motivational tape?"

Jessica had been so preoccupied she hadn't noticed Tanya had stepped up to her locker a few spaces down and was now looking at her in a way that made Jessica wish she *had* been wearing earphones and carrying a pocket recorder. Embarrassed, she smiled and shook her head. "You caught me. The secret's out— Jessica Holland's going off the deep end."

"Guess you had a pretty rough night, huh?" Tanya asked sympathetically.

"Do I look that bad?"

"I wouldn't say 'bad.' You should see me when I catch a cold. But you do look as though it won't be hard for one of the supervisors to catch you sleeping on your feet. Anyway, I've been worrying about you. The way you left here yesterday—"

"Tanya, I'm sorry about that," Jessica said quickly. "I know you must think I came off sounding like a first-class witch. Let's blame it on my Taurus temperament. Normally I can keep it under control, but I suppose I let it slip away from me yesterday."

"An apology is unnecessary. Under the circumstances, I think I would have reacted the same way. How can men be so dense about certain things?"

Jessica shut her locker door and shot the doe-eyed woman beside her a grateful look. "If you ever find out the answer, let me know."

"Though, if you ask me, I still think things will turn out all right."

Unwilling to broach the subject further, Jessica said, "I think it's great that you and Marco are seeing each other. Okay," she amended, noting Tanya's lifted eyebrow. "I'll admit I was shocked at first, but I really am happy for you."

"I think I'm still somewhat shocked myself." Tanya's eyes twinkled as she rummaged in her own locker. "Up until now my dates were usually low-keyed, hardly what you would call flamboyant types. Marco can be quite a character when he puts his mind to it."

"You mean it's not a permanent condition?" Jessica gasped, earning a chuckle from her friend.

"I thought that, too, when I first met him. Do you know on our first date he took me to the marine park? I don't think we were there two hours before he was putting on his own show doing magic tricks for a pack of cub scouts at a concession stand."

"He does like kids."

"And—ugh—pineapple on his cereal... playing puttputt golf when it's drizzling, because he says it's less crowded... He just enjoys being spontaneous. Don't you adore that in a man?"

Jessica's answering shrug was more of a tightening of her shoulder muscles. "I, um, don't really know. Ben's not exactly what you'd call spontaneous."

"Well, they can surprise you sometimes," Tanya replied, her expression turning thoughtful. "Do you know Marco almost got his ear pierced once? But thank goodness he had the good sense to think about what the chief of staff would say."

"A lot probably," Jessica drawled, chuckling.

Tanya's eyes grew dreamy. "He's so sweet and thoughtful. He's the most romantic man I've ever met." Seeing Jessica's smile wilt, Tanya groaned in distress. "What an idiot I am. I shouldn't have brought that up now when you're feeling as depressed as you are."

"Why not? I enjoy hearing that you're happy. My goodness, I can't expect the world to stop revolving just because of my little disappointments." Aware that Tanya might be able to see that her blitheness was all bravado, she busied herself with making sure her hair was neatly clipped back and her hat was secured. Sure enough, it wasn't long before her friend spoke up.

"Jessie. I really hate to see you hurting like this. What can I do to help?"

"Well, how about considering sharing my apartment with me? I've been meaning to talk to you about it for a while now. It's a two-bedroom unit with plenty of space and it's close to the hospital."

"It does sound wonderful. I'm not at all happy where I am, but don't you think this is a bit premature?"

"I know you and I haven't known each other that long, but—" She stopped, realizing she must have misunderstood. "Are you saying you and Marco might be—? No, not this soon."

"You've got that right. While I'm tempted to hope this might be the real thing, I'm in no hurry." Tanya reached over to touch Jessica's arm. "I was talking about you and Dr. Collier. Just because you two had a misunderstanding doesn't mean it's over between you."

"Tanya, I'm tired of trying to convince him that what I feel for him isn't some childish infatuation. I give up."

"After seeing how you are with him, Jessie, and then watching him yesterday when you walked out, there's no denying there are deep feelings between you two," Tanya said gently. "Do you really think you can give up?"

"I have to try."

Tanya gave her friend's shoulder a sympathetic squeeze and, promising to talk to her again at break, left to get to her own station. It was then that Jessica noticed the slim black ribbon tied to her left arm. She wanted to ask her about it, but Tanya was already heading out the women's changing room; besides, a quick glance at her watch told her she'd had to hustle herself if she was going to get up to her floor on time.

As expected, the other nurses greeted her warmly but were full of questions when she checked in at the nursing station. Jessica assured them that Ben had indeed regained his sight and hedged the more personal questions as best she could. She did, however, notice that several of them were wearing the ribbons. When she had a chance, she drew aside a young nurse named Sallye and asked if someone on the staff had passed away.

"Oh, no. It's nothing like that," Sallye replied with a wide grin.

"That's a relief. So what is it, a gag for a fortieth birthday or something?"

"Yeah, something like that."

Jessica was about to ask the name of the poor soul, who was obviously in for a terrible ribbing, but Sallye quickly excused herself saying she had to run some blood tests downstairs to the lab. As she hurried to catch an elevator, Jessica turned to ask one of the other nurses and spotted Marco coming down the hall. He, too, was wearing a ribbon.

"Hey, Jesserooni. I heard you put yourself back on the front lines." But after giving her a friendly wink, he tilted his head and scowled as he studied the faint shadows she knew were under her eyes. "Hmm... maybe you rushed things. You don't look like you had a great night."

"I've had better, but I'll be all right. I didn't have a chance to ask Tanya earlier about how things went yesterday. How was the examination?"

"Whose?" Marco asked innocently.

"Don't tease me this morning," she pleaded. "You know perfectly well whose. Ben's."

"Why the curiosity? The way you flew out of here I figured you'd be about ready to be introduced to my younger brother, Dylan. Did I ever tell you about him? He owns a pet store on the other side of town. Great guy—not as good-looking as me, but a terrific personality.''

"Marco—will you please just tell me? Did Ben's vision clear completely? Did he need stitches? What about his ribs? Did the fall reinjure them?''

He raised his hands palm out to stop her. "Yes to the first question and no to everything else. He's going to have one heck of a knot on his head for a few days, but the scratch was just a bleeder. On a more interesting note, would you care to hear what he said when he walked into his condominium and found you'd already packed and left?''

"You went with him?''

"Dear heart, you left the man stranded. Someone had to see he made it home. Anyway, lucky for you I have the exclusive play-by-play right up here," he said tapping his forehead.

"I don't want to hear it, thank you," Jessica said quickly. "I was merely concerned with his health.'' She dropped her gaze to the black ribbon. "Who's turning forty?''

"Forty?'' Marco glanced down at his sleeve and broke into a devilish grin. "Is that what everyone's been telling you? Great, then let me be the first to give you the inside scoop. Ben's handing them out.''

Jessica nearly dropped the clipboard she was holding. "Ben's *here*? But he's not supposed to be. He isn't well enough to put in a full day. How could you let him?''

"Calm down," Marco replied, giving her a reassuring pat on the back. "First of all, he's not working, he's only touching bases with the chief of staff,

Wescott and a few others. He doesn't plan to return to a full-time schedule until next week. Second, even if I'd tried to persuade him to stay home, he wouldn't have listened to me. The man's clearly on a mission. Suddenly he's become immune to anything remotely resembling logic. It's rather refreshing, if I may say so myself."

"I don't understand a word you're saying. Are you going to tell me *why* he gave you that ribbon or aren't you?"

Marco's expression turned suspiciously innocent. "He's asked several of us to join him in mourning his broken heart."

"He didn't."

"You doubt it?"

"I doubt that it was his idea. Marco, how could you? You know Ben isn't someone who willingly draws attention to himself."

"Then why did he ask me to help him pass these out?"

Jessica stared at him, unable to decide if she should believe him or not. "He did? Are you sure?"

"Positive—and I wonder what it all means," Marco drawled as he inspected his close-clipped fingernails.

"He's obviously having a bad reaction to his medication."

"Jessie, we took him off the last of his medication before he left the hospital, remember?"

Deciding she had no intention of becoming the laughingstock of the entire building, Jessica narrowed her eyes. "Where is he?"

"Last I noticed, he and Wescott were heading for the lounge. Hey!" he said when she whipped the ribbon from his arm. "I look good in black. Take someone else's."

"I plan to," she said, making a beeline for the next person she saw wearing one and, stopping them, she held out her hand expectantly.

One by one everyone handed them over. Some grinned while doing it, others asked, tongue in cheek, if they could follow and watch when she handed them to Ben. Finally, when she had collected what she hoped was all of them, she headed for the lounge.

She was reaching for the door when it suddenly opened. Reaching out to protect her face, she dropped the ribbons. "Blast," she muttered, stooping to scoop them up.

About to rise, she noticed the conservative, laced-up shoes of the man standing before her. Something about them was uncomfortably familiar and had her looking upward along gray slacks that had an immaculately crisp seam, up the doctor's lab coat to the bright red heart pinned to the pocket and a brief though inflammatory message scrawled across it.

Jessie Holland broke my heart.

Sucking in a quick breath, she glanced up at Ben's face. He was watching her intently. Twin spots of bright color stained his cheeks. She understood the color; no doubt he was in agony over wearing something so outrageous. His intense look, however, needed some explaining.

Quickly collecting the ribbons, she rose. "All right, Ben...what's going on?" she demanded, her voice shaking with nerves and indignation.

Ben stared at Jessie, wondering when he'd ever seen her looking more lovely. Granted, her expression wasn't encouraging, but her skin had a glow from yesterday's time spent in the sun. It was particularly attractive against the crisp white of her uniform and her always striking dark hair. And despite the faint shadows under her eyes that made him hope she hadn't slept any better than he did, their moss-green color was every bit as intriguing as he remembered.

He wondered if she realized how close he was to dragging her into his arms and kissing her, consequences be damned. Considering the anguish she'd put him through last night, who would really blame him? But as someone slipped around them to get into the lounge, he realized that he'd pushed his luck far enough already and, instead of answering her, carefully led her away from the doorway.

"Ben...please."

"Give me a second. Do you realize this is the first time I've really had a chance to look at you since I was blinded? Really look at you, I mean. It makes me want to count my blessings all over again," he murmured gruffly.

Jessie looked away and raised a hand to fiddle with her collar. "Why—um—why did you do all this?"

"I thought it would be a good way to get your attention."

"Oh, it was that all right. Mine and everyone else's in this place."

Ben rubbed the area of his forehead just beneath his newest bandage. Somehow this wasn't going the way he'd visualized it. "You don't think it was spontaneous?"

"I didn't say that."

"Or romantic?"

Jessie stared at him for a full five seconds before shaking her head. "What do you want from me, Ben?"

Back on track, Ben thought with relief, and he relaxed to where he could smile. "To start with—how about fifty years of your semi-undivided attention?" Unfortunately a nurse and two interns were passing at that precise moment. Ben didn't know who looked more stunned, them or Jessie. The nurse and interns broke into ear-to-ear grins; Jessie looked as if she was going to need an IV at any second. Concerned, Ben reached for her. "Would you like to sit down? You'd better sit down," he said more decisively.

Taking her arm, he led her to a bench a few yards away, suddenly wishing the potted plant beside it was about three times its current size. He would have given a lot to have a modicum of privacy right now. The ribbons had been one thing, but this wasn't exactly the spot where he'd planned to have this scene with Jessie.

"On second thought," he began, "maybe we could go someplace less congested."

"I can't leave. I'm on duty until five," Jessie told him. She stared hard at the red heart. "Would you mind repeating what you said a moment ago?"

"I said I wanted to spend the next fifty or so years with you," he said with quiet earnestness.

"And the part about having my semi-undivided attention?"

"Well," he risked another smile, "children do demand their share, don't they?"

Jessie nodded, though she still looked somewhat dazed. "Is this a proposal?"

Swallowing, Ben tried to find his voice. Why did they always make it look so damned easy in the movies? Why wasn't she responding to him the way she did that night in his kitchen? Of course then it had been dark and he hadn't felt as if a hundred pairs of eyes were peering at him from every corner. Damn! He'd meant to handle this with more style. She deserved some style.

"Yes," he said forcefully.

"That's it?"

As her eyebrows lifted into haughty arcs, Ben felt his strategy do a major belly flop. Didn't she realize he'd never done this before in his life, never even *wanted* to until now, and that he was afraid? Not of the commitment, because he already knew in his heart that heaven couldn't guarantee him enough years to make Jessie as happy as she deserved to be. But he was afraid of it not being enough. He could give her security and a nice life-style—even a guaranteed set of loving in-laws who'd been waiting for him to do this for a long time.

But was he going to be able to give her spring in January and laughter when problems arose? She was so full of life, so vibrant; would she continue to thrive with him or would she awaken one morning and realize she was being suffocated by his boringness?

"Oh, God," Jessie whispered, dropping her gaze to her clenched hands. "Do you think I want to hear words you have to force out of your mouth? Do you think I want you to wear hearts and ribbons and do things that I know you're not comfortable with because you think *I* want them? I fell in love with *you*, not some caricature of a person you think will please me." She jumped to her feet and thrust the ribbons into his hands. "I'm sorry you went through all the trouble."

Jessica almost broke into a run, knowing if she didn't hurry, she was going to burst into tears. But she got no farther than a few feet when she was whirled around and thrust back against the wall. She found herself staring into Ben's face; not the Ben who'd just succeeded in breaking her heart for the second time in twenty-four hours, but one whose wonderful gray eyes glinted with temper and passion; one whose facial muscles looked stretched so tautly she could see a blood vessel pulsating at his temple. One who made her bite back the words of anger she'd been about to fling at him.

"I love you," he ground out, his gaze intense and unwavering. "Do you hear me? Not because I feel obligated or because I'm trying to sound trendy. I *love* you because that's the way it is."

"Ben—" Over his shoulder Jessica saw that a nurse's aide and the patient she was escorting had decided to stop and watch them. "You don't have to do this. You're absolutely right, this isn't the right place anyway."

"Now who's flubbing their lines?" he murmured, dropping his gaze to her lips. "I guess I'll just have to force the right ones out of you."

He kissed her and silenced the words of protest she'd been about to say. It had been too long since he'd done this anyway, she admitted to herself in resignation. She was certain she would have died if he hadn't held her again, kissed her. Even as she felt herself go warm and mellow against him, she knew that she wouldn't be able to walk away.

"Jessie," he whispered.

He showed her in his kiss what he'd meant to with his words, what Jessie realized he wanted to do with his hands. When he cupped her face, Jessie understood all the tenderness and need he was feeling. Her heart filled as did her eyes.

She didn't have to doubt it any longer. He truly loved her.

When he raised his head, Jessie smiled at him through her tears of joy. "Well?" he demanded with tender gruffness. "Am I going to hear it or not?"

"I love you, Ben."

"I want more than that, darling."

For a second she looked confused, then she broke into a radiant smile. "I adore you, Dr. Benedict Collier . . . and I would be honored to be your wife."

This time their kiss was more urgent as the final walls they'd been holding between them crashed down and were swept away in a warm tide of loving.

When they parted again, they were breathing even more unsteadily than before. Jessica thought she could drown in the depth of emotions she saw in Ben's eyes and she hoped he was seeing something equally profound in hers.

"Soon?" he asked.

She nodded with an eagerness that had her ponytail bouncing on her back. "As soon as you'd like."

"Don't tempt me," he groaned. "Once I make my mind up about something, I have this tendency to suffer tunnel vision."

"Tell me about it." She chuckled, smoothing back his hair adoringly. But a glance over his shoulder brought the discovery that their audience had grown considerably. "Oh, dear . . . um, Ben . . ."

"In a second. Just one more kiss," he said, gently pressing his mouth to hers.

"Dr. Collier," came a stern voice from behind them. "Would you mind explaining what's going on here?"

Jessica gasped then almost had heart failure when she recognized the chief of staff. Dr. Lowe was a slender, small man with unemotional blue eyes and an inclination for biting criticism. Most of the hospital staff were terrified of him and she was no exception.

She hastily wiped a smudge of lipstick off Ben's lips before he turned to face him. When he slipped his hand behind his back, Jessica gratefully took it and clung tightly.

"Why I'm proposing, sir," Ben explained genially.

The comment as well as this demonstration of affection was so far away from everyone's perception of the somber and studious Dr. Collier that not only did half the people standing around guffaw, but even Dr. Lowe bowed his head to cover a smile.

"Ahem. Yes, I see," Lowe replied. "And, er, has the young lady accepted?"

Ben turned to Jessie and cocked an eyebrow. She gulped. "Y-yes, sir."

"Fine. Fine. In that case, do you two think you could move the celebrating elsewhere, preferably someplace less central to our staff and patients?"

"Of course, sir," Ben said. "Right away."

The senior physician began to turn away and then paused. "On second thought, why don't you go on out there somewhere?" he said, wagging his hand toward the window at the end of the hall. "If memory serves, you're both still supposed to be on leave anyway, am I correct?"

"Correct," Ben said quickly.

"Then move along before this traffic jam becomes chronic."

"Yes, *sir,*" they replied in unison.

As soon as Dr. Lowe rounded a corner, their audience broke into applause. Several interns indulged in low-keyed whistles, and while Jessie got a number of hugs, Ben received his share of backslaps.

When they were finally alone again, Ben let out a boyish whoop and hugged Jessie, rocking her back and forth. Then he smiled into her eyes. "You heard the man. We have to vacate the premises."

"How could he have known that?" she asked awed. "I mean, knowing about you is one thing, but me? He's never said more to me than 'hello' or 'down please' if we met in an elevator."

"Ah-ah." Ben touched his finger to her lips. "Don't underestimate yourself, my dear. You're a fine nurse and *everyone* here knows it, including Dr. Lowe. Most importantly, however, I think he was recognizing that you're about to become Mrs. Collier and to keep *me* happily affiliated with this hospital he has to keep *you* happy."

"Mrs. Collier... oh, I like the sound of that," Jessica whispered.

"Good. Now tell me what you think of this. I see a long leisurely brunch in our future, followed by a shopping expedition to various jewelry stores for the perfect engagement ring. Then," he added stroking her cheek, "a candlelit dinner down at the River Walk at the restaurant of your choice."

Jessica reached up to give Ben a light kiss before linking her arm with his. "Doctor, let me lead the way."

MORE ABOUT
THE VIRGO MAN

by Lydia Lee

When it comes to the Virgo man, we might as well cover his flaws as quickly as possible so we can get on to his virtues. Wait a minute. Virgo...flawed? And you thought he was perfection personified! Well, maybe that last one you dated was as neat as a pin, courteous, on time, a health nut and even had his spice rack alphabetized. Still, if you cast your mind back, you'll also remember that he had this devastating habit of criticizing you, he wasn't really all that romantic, and when he left your life, there was an icy finality. You still get the shivers just thinking about it. So, yes, Virgos *are* flawed. But there are ways around this earthbound, practical sign. There are also a few unsung attributes that his modesty and natural reserve have kept well hidden.

The first thing you'd better know is that if you're looking for a dashing lover who'll sweep you off into Never-Never Land, you'd do better with an Aries or a Leo. Virgos are not wired that way. This isn't to say he's immune to romance or passion; far from it. Once committed, your Virgoan can burn with quite a bit of voltage. And the nice thing about him is, unlike the bonfire type who is here today and long gone tomorrow, his is a steady, nurturing heat. That's all well and good, you're probably saying by now. You weren't interested in a lot of razzle-dazzle anyway. You actually like his refined approach to lovemaking, but living with a full-time critic? The solution? Laugh it off! Turn the other cheek. Realize this is his way of letting you know he cares. Smile and say thank you, then let him go back to his drafting board, or to puttering in the attic with his model train set. Once he's had his say and been acknowledged, he'll happily return to whatever it was he was doing. And Virgos are always doing something!

If a Virgo man has caught your eye, and you're wondering what to do to catch his, realize that this one takes his time almost as much as a Taurus does. Only with him, it's not that he's slow to act, it's that he's extremely discerning. He's looking for an intelligent, classy woman. You can forget about that black leather outfit with the tasseled boots. More than anything, your Mercury-ruled man wants a quality relationship, and if you fit the bill, he'll find a way to let you know. So be patient. He can be brought around.

Remember though, this man is subtle and very particular. Some astrologers advise women interested in Virgos to be neat. That fly-away hair and plaids-with-stripes outfit will drive him bonkers. Or perhaps it will present a worthy challenge: at last, someone he can really help. Professor Higgins, meet Eliza Doolittle!

This brings us to the final area concerning Virgos, which is probably one of the reasons they like to fuss so much over you. They were put on this planet to work and be of service. A little bit of worrying actually makes them happy. They shine in any of the healing professions: doctor, nurse, therapist. They also excel at anything requiring detailed work and make superb architects, draftsmen and engineers. However, that urge to fix *you* will pop up, so don't be surprised when he gives you his unsolicited opinion concerning that cold you can't get rid of.

But where is the romance? some of you might still be asking. Rest assured, it's still there. It's quiet and unassuming and, oddly enough, at times even a little poetic. Though you can probably forget being serenaded at your balcony, look, instead, for someone who really will care for you in sickness and health. Look for a man who's faithful, hardworking, sometimes a little cranky but gentle and tender, too. This is the kind of man who'll love you as much in his own quiet way on your fiftieth wedding anniversary as he did when you first met. So what if he doesn't promise you the moon. What on earth would you do with it anyway?

*   *   *   *   *

FAMOUS VIRGO MEN

Peter Sellers
Maurice Chevalier
H. G. Wells
Peter Falk
Leo Tolstoy

COMING NEXT MONTH

#820 PILLOW TALK—Patricia Ellis
Written in the Stars
Kendall Arden had made a big mistake in getting involved with
Jared Dalton's research on sleep. How could she confess her sensual
dreams to this oh-so-dedicated Libra man? Especially since he was the
subject of her fantasies....

#821 AND DADDY MAKES THREE—Anne Peters
Eric Schwenker firmly believed that a mother's place was at home, so why
was Isabel Mott using *his* office to care for her daughter? Maybe Isabel
could teach him about working mothers...and what a family truly was.

#822 CASEY'S FLYBOY—Vivian Leiber
Cautious Casey Stevens knew what she wanted—a decent, *civilized* home
for her baby. But sexy flyboy Leon Brodie tempted her to spread her wings
and fly. The handsome pilot was a good reason to let herself soar....

#823 PAPER MARRIAGE—Judith Bowen
Justine O'Malley was shocked by rancher Clayton Truscott's marriage
proposal—but then, so was he. Clayton had sworn never to trust a woman
again. But to keep his brother's children, he would do anything—
even *marry!*

#824 BELOVED STRANGER—Peggy Webb
Belinda Stubaker was incensed! Her employer, Reeve Lawrence, was
acting like Henry Higgins—insisting on teaching her the finer things in
life. How could Belinda explain to Reeve that *love* was the finest thing
there was....

#825 HOME FOR THANKSGIVING—Suzanne Carey
One kiss, so many years ago. Now, Dr. Aaron Dash and Kendra Jenkins
were colleagues at the same hospital. But that kiss could never be
forgotten. Beneath their professionalism, an intense passion
still lingered....

AVAILABLE THIS MONTH: